# WORKHOUSE GIRL & THE VEILED LADY

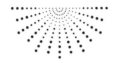

## DOLLY PRICE

© 2020 PUREREAD LTD

PUREREAD.COM

# CONTENTS

# CHAPTER ONE

Perhaps it's just as well nobody remembers the day they were born, to spare the feelings of those whose births cause disappointment. On a spring day in 1850, Albert Coomb dreamed of a baby boy while he stoked the fires of the *Adonis*, the packet that travelled the regular route between Liverpool and New York. He would not know until he returned to his home port that his bride Maureen had given him a girl.

In Liverpool on a fresh April morning, his daughters from his first marriage, aged twelve and ten, decided that their new sister, bald and pink like a piglet, was hardly worth a look. They had wanted a brother, not a sister.

Mrs. Coomb, the quiet twenty-year-old woman who had married the widower fifteen years her senior, cried at first upon being told that the child was a girl. She had rashly promised her husband a son. She had told him she was sure!

Albert Coomb's parents, who lived a few streets away from Crescent Court, had loved their son's first wife, Roberta. They'd even bought a house with money inherited from Albert's great-uncle who made a tidy bit and never married. The house was a two-up, two-down terraced in a quiet Court. They allowed the young couple to live there paying only a token rent. How wise of them not to have *given* Bertie the house—his father had been against that, because you don't ever know what the future might bring. Alfred was proved correct—Roberta died and now this young chit Maureen was mistress of it!

After Bertie had lost his first wife five years ago, the older Coombs had taken in the girls and let the house. When he'd remarried, they couldn't say no to his having it again, at the same low rent, even though they disapproved of his choice.

They had been relieved of the care of the two girls after he had remarried, so they were happy about that, for Sally and Debra were a handful for the old couple. They were stubborn, hot-headed children.

They'd have preferred a sensible widow for Bertie, a woman with knowledge of the world, who knew how to manage her housekeeping money, who could control her stepdaughters, and a purse of money wouldn't have hurt either. Maureen O'Brien was young, a poor immigrant. She seemed careless and vague. What great good luck she had, to have a house to live in, and she so young, and not long arrived from Ireland! As a bride, old Mrs. Coomb had had to make do with a room at first, then two rooms, then half-a-house—she'd never had a house all to herself. By rights they should move in, but their objection to Maureen, and living again with Sally and Debra, ruled it out.

Added to her other faults, Bertie's new wife could not even give him a son. Here was another girl for him to feed while he waited for his beloved male child.

"At least she's healthy," remarked Mrs. Coomb, looking in at the sleeping babe.

"Oh, she's a little dote, no trouble at all!" said her daughter-in-law fondly from her bed.

Maureen had been cured of her disappointment very rapidly. One look at her daughter, her first-born, and her tears had vanished. She was besotted now with Olivia Mary Coomb. She was completely beautiful. She had downy fuzz on her head and her skin was a healthy pink. And if Bertie was cross about the baby not being a boy, pity about him—she loved her baby girl.

"How long will your cousin be able ter stay, Maureen?"

"I don't know. She'll stay as long as she can, I'm sure."

Mrs. Coomb sighed to herself and wondered why she had bothered asking. It was impossible for Maureen to give straight answers. To expect her to say 'Monday,' or 'next week' or even 'next month' was futile.

"I had better be going 'ome," she said then. "Drink beef tea, Maureen, and eat liver. That's what I always did after the children were born, and I didn't need to lie-in more than a week."

Maureen's cousin, Mrs. Dowling, came upstairs just then, and offered tea, which the older woman refused. She'd had Mrs. Dowling's tea before. Her husband was fond of remarking that it was so strong you could race horses across it. She took her shawl from the back of her chair and wound herself up in it to face the stiff breeze coming from the Mersey.

# CHAPTER TWO

"Mother, the *Adonis* is back in port!" Debra ran into the house. She had run ahead of Sally, who wanted to wait for her father to disembark. The girls called her 'Mother' because their father had told them to. Maureen found it strange to be called mother to two strapping lasses when she was so young herself.

"Oh, it's early so. They must have had the tide. Debra, wash the dishes in the basin." Maureen was placidly feeding her three-week-old baby. If it had been a boy, his name was to have been Albert Patrick, and since she had been so certain of the baby's sex, she and Albert had not even thought of a girl's name.

She liked the name Olivia. She had heard it once on the docks, when she had been selling fruit from her barrow. A posh woman had been walking by, with a little girl all dressed up in a blue velvet coat and white boots. Long flaxen ringlets peeped out from under her lacy blue hat. She had big bow under her chin, and rosy cheeks. Maureen had taken to her and held out an apple for her. The little girl had run up to her, her hand outstretched. Her mother had called out *'Olivia! Come back here!'* and the little girl had obeyed. The girl Olivia had come and gone like a ship in the night, but the pretty name had stayed with Maureen. *If I ever have a daughter,* she'd thought to herself, *I'll call her Olivia. Olivia Mary. Mary after my mother, God rest her soul.* Now she had her daughter, and she pictured her at four years old, exactly like the other Olivia, though where she would ever get the money for white boots and a blue velvet coat, she did not know. Giving her the name of a rich girl showed a hope that she would never be in want.

Debra did not want to do the wash-up, so she ran out again to meet her father and Sally coming up from the landing stage. Maureen was mildly annoyed, but she'd make her do it when she came back, her and Sally. They were bold, impudent girls.

Of course, she felt sorry for them losing their mother so early in life, but that didn't excuse their determination to go their own way and not mind anyone. They had a girl coming in every day to do the hard scrubbing, but Maureen did everything else.

Well, she couldn't be expected to take the girls in hand. Another few years, and they'd be working and then married. That day couldn't come soon enough for Maureen. She had her own darling girl to look after. Olivia wouldn't turn out like those two. What bad example!

The door opened a while later, and Bertie came in with his daughters. He was handsome for his age, his dark hair sprinkled with grey in only a few places, his face that of a sailor, brown and rugged.

He swung his kit onto the chair.

"So it's another girl," he said flatly.

"Now don't blame me for the first two," answered Maureen with a smile, but a wink at Debra in an effort to take the harm out of it. "But Bertie, I thought it was a boy, because Mrs. Lang did the ring test over my stomach. It spun around and around. But never mind—isn't she bonny, Bertie?"

"I suppose she is. Have you any food ready for me?" he asked plaintively, while Sally and Debra rummaged through his belongings to see if he had brought any New York candies.

"I have mutton stew we can heat up on the fire. But aren't you pleased, Bertie?" Maureen asked in an appealing tone.

"I'm pleased you came through it all right. And—that the babe is a healthy one." He added grudgingly. "The house is an awful mess."

"It is, because your daughters won't obey me."

"We do!" the girls chorused. "Don't believe her, Papa!"

"Your grandmother used to say the same thing," he growled to them.

"Go and get the stew and put it on the fire," said Maureen to Sally. She scowled but did as she was told. The only time those girls did anything for her was when their father was around.

Over the next day or so, until it was time for him to leave again, Bertie had time to see that this was a more placid baby than either of the others, and he left, getting fond of her, and hoping that the *next* child would be a boy. He left Maureen with most of his wages, as always. He was a very good provider.

# CHAPTER THREE

Baby Olivia, at four weeks old, already had a head of dark hair and a friend. This was Julia Sullivan, her next-door neighbour. The Sullivans had moved into Crescent Court only two months before Olivia was born. Julia had been born shortly after they'd moved in and like Olivia, was a happy, thriving baby. She had several older brothers and sisters. They were a noisy, happy bunch, and Mrs. Sullivan thought that, as she was now forty-two years old, Julia would always be the baby.

Mrs. Sullivan liked her young neighbour who was the same age as her oldest daughter, but looked even younger, as she was very petite and had a naïve look in spite of the hardships she had suffered. She took her under her wing. There was nothing Mrs.

Sullivan didn't know about infant care and feeding. Her house was awash in all kinds of baby items from small cups and spoons to potties and clouts and pins, gowns and bonnets in all sizes and many of these were finding their way next door.

"The poor woman, she's hardly more than a child herself," Mrs. Sullivan said to her husband one evening when he was questioning why another armful of linen was leaving the house. "Apart from that cousin who lives in London, and a brother—but what use is a man to a new mother—she has nobody in this country at all. Her in-laws look down on her. As for the husband, he barely spoke to her when he last came from New York. You'll have to talk to 'im, Fred. Tell him there are a lot more years for 'im to get a son."

"Din't he leave her enough money to buy all she needed for the baby?" Mr. Sullivan was indignant. He worked as a ship's chandler. He knew plenty of sailors and had a poor opinion of many of them, who used their shore leave to get drunk and cause trouble. He had heard a great deal more about Bertie Coomb than Mrs. Sullivan suspected, but he kept it to himself. It might only be gossip. "He has regular work on the New York packet steamer, and should 'ave left her enough."

"It's her first. She didn't know what she needed, and we won't be needing these again, I hope. There's some more tea in the pot, if you want it." She scooped up Julia in her arms and shouting for her son Tommy to open the front door for her, she disappeared into the street.

The two babies were placed side by side in the cot while the mothers chatted. Mrs. Sullivan, also from Ireland, had come over twenty-five years ago. Work was plentiful here in Liverpool for her hardworking husband, and he had recently been promoted. They'd never had much; this had been their first house all to themselves, and she was very proud of it, though the rent was a lot, it was great not to have to share the stairs with all kinds of people, some of them rascals and reprobates, too fond of beer and the women partial to gin.

The two babies lay side by side, awake, and seemingly perfectly content, while their mothers drank cups of tea.

"They'll be like twins," predicted Mrs. Sullivan. "Maureen, don't you know she's still too young for a pillow." She got up and took the little pillow from under Olivia's head.

Maureen didn't mind at all that Mrs. Sullivan directed her mothering practises and chided her for doing the wrong things.

There was a short rap at the door, before the visitor opened it and walked in.

"It's my brother, you 'avent met him yet, Bertha. Come in, Jimmy!" A man some years older than Maureen, lean of form but with a broad, smiling face and twinkling eyes, had entered the living-room and doffed his hat, hanging it on a nail beside the door.

"God save all here," he said, grinning. "I was relieved to hear you're all right and the babby too. We've had enough dyin' in our family." He came to the cot.

"Two of 'em!"

"One of 'em is mine," crowed Mrs. Sullivan. "Don't mix 'em up on us!"

"This one's an O'Brien." Jimmy said, putting his finger into the little fist of the Sullivan child, who was bigger and more plump than Olivia.

"Go on with you, you chancer! That's Mrs. Sullivan's baby!"

"All babies look the same." he said, to take a rise out of the women. He was rewarded with an exasperated chorus of protest in return.

Jimmy worked as a labourer at Waterloo Docks. Maureen was his only surviving sister, and it was on his account she had come to England after the rest of the family perished in the Irish Potato Famine a few years before. The Great Hunger had claimed their parents and two brothers.

# CHAPTER FOUR

The following year, Mr. Coomb had his longed-for son, and two years after, a second. John and William delighted him, and he forgot that Olivia had any claim to his love. She hardly noticed. Her father was rarely at home, and Uncle Jimmy, on his visits, captured her heart. She loved the lively, chatty man who, whenever he visited, always put laughter in the house. And Uncle Jimmy often brought her to the bakery owned by Mr. Moser.

The Mosers were in Liverpool by accident. Many years ago, on their way from Austria to a new life in America, they'd been robbed of everything they owned by a gang of 'magsmen' whose speciality was thieving from travellers. Hoping that the dock police would be able to find their belongings, Mr. Moser sold the tickets for their voyage to another family. But the thieves were never found. Their money was soon spent on food and lodgings, and with poor English and six children to feed, the family was in deep trouble. Mr Moser began work in a bakery owned by Mr Darby, and Mrs. Moser as a maid in the Darby house, while their eldest daughter minded the other children in their very humble rooms. Mr. Moser's skills with Viennese pastry began to draw more customers into the little bakery than ever before. After two years they had saved enough money for the steerage fare to America, but by that time, the warm and irrepressible spirits of the Liverpudlians had overcome them, and they could not bear to leave all those who had helped a family in great trouble, even if the trouble had been caused by Liverpool criminals. The New World was forgotten. Mr. Moser planned to strike out on his own, but rather than let him go, Mr. Darby offered him shares in the business. Mr. Darby retired some years later, and Mr. Moser bought him out.

Moser's cinnamon snails—long, curly sticks finished by a knob at one end with two raisins for eyes— were very popular with little customers, though they had a long German name that only the Mosers knew. Olivia loved them and Uncle Jimmy bought three for a penny, which she ate in the shop, starting at the end of the snail and working her way to the head, which was her favourite bit. Julia, when she came with them, liked to eat the head first.

Moser's Bakery was Olivia's favourite place in all of Liverpool.

In time, Sally and then Debra began work at the chocolate factory, Chandelier Chocolates in Old Hall Street. It was owned by a businessman named Slater. Nobody knew how the name Chandelier Chocolates came about, but people supposed that Slater wished to appeal to the upper-class clientele with his choice.

"If they'd wanted to appeal to us, they'd 'ave called it Smoking Gaslamp Chocolates." Mrs. Sullivan chortled. "But it must be a fancy place. How do Sally and Debra like it there?"

"They hate it. It might sound fancy an' all, but it's not very nice inside. The Roasting Room is very hot. And they have to work long hours, and I never see much of their wages, though they live here and eat the food I cook," said Maureen, dandling Baby Willie on her lap. "Those girls do nothing but complain about their lot. I can't wait for 'em to get married."

"They're horrid to Olivia," she said in a whisper, for the little girl was running about the living-room, playing tag with Julia. "They don't just ignore her. If she as much as touches a hairpin belonging to them, they're running to me to complain."

"That's a shame."

"Her father hasn't any interest in her. Her grandparents don't care. The only love she gets is from my side. Jimmy for instance. He's stone mad about her, and she him."

"Julia loves 'im too! It's his stories, and his way with little ones. He comes down to their level, and never lords it over them."

"Even Sally and Debra like him, and that's saying something, cos they don't like anybody."

"People who smile as much as he does spread joy around," was Mrs. Sullivan's opinion. "He should have a brood of his own. Will he ever marry, do you think?"

"There was a girl long ago," said Maureen. "He never speaks of her. His heart got broken, though you'd never think it, to look at him laugh and chat as if he 'adn't a care in the world. He's ten years older than me, and went away to work when I was a small child, so I never really knew him until I came over here. Her name was Lily."

"Well it's high time he got over her! He's young yet, Maureen."

Their chat was interrupted by John, who had spent the last while playing tag with the girls, though all he knew of the game was to run around in circles emitting loud shouts with all the noise his two-year-old lungs could muster.

"Stop it, Johnny!" cried Maureen at last. "I'll go deaf! Come here, lad, and play with Willie."

"I'd better be getting home," Mrs. Sullivan said. "I have bread on the fire, and Deirdre will forget to look at it." She wound her cloak around her, told Julia to follow, and they left.

Maureen knew it was time to get the girls' supper, but she didn't know what to give them. No matter what they got, they always would prefer something else.

## CHAPTER FIVE

"I wonder what she 'as for us tonight," said Sally, walking briskly along the street. "I hope it's something better than bread and cheese. I didn't eat any of the liver she gave us yesterday. It was overdone."

"When you get married, Sally, I'm coming to live with you. And you better hurry up about it. I can't wait to get away from her."

"Married!" Sally tossed her head. "When I marry, it'll be to a man with a fortune."

"You're pretty enough to attract any man you want." Debra said. "And he better have a brother. We'll be made up, you and me!"

"I have someone in mind, Debra."

"Who, sister, who?"

"The man who rides by us on the brown mare every day around this time—Mr. Longman!"

"That's Mr. Slater's nephew! And 'e isn't 'andsome, Sally. You'd 'ave to look at his long droopy moustache for the rest of your life, you would."

"He can shave it off, Debra." Sally said loftily, glancing up and down the street before she and her sister stepped across it. "He's very shy, and thinks nothing of himself. He'll always have a good position with Chandelier Chocolates. Don't you see the way he looks at me, when he passes through the room? I will be one of *The Family*, Debra! You watch me."

"But can I come and live with you, Sally? Don't say no!"

"Of course, you can! Do you think I'd let you stay in Crescent Court? Oh, look, look, here he comes! Take my arm, pretend I've just hurt my ankle."

Sally bent and rubbed her ankle, holding on to her sister, her face drawn in mock pain. To her secret delight, Mr. Longman stopped.

"Are you hurt, Miss -em—? May I be of use?"

"Oh thank you, I'm Miss Coomb—"

"I ought to know your name, for you work for my uncle." He tipped his hat.

"I'm just one of many girls who work in the Roasting Room, Mr. Longman. You couldn't know all of us by name. This is my sister, Miss Debra."

Mr. Longman bowed his head politely, then dismounted his horse.

"I twisted it, but I think I'll be all right," Sally said bravely, biting her lip.

"You cannot walk, Miss Coomb." Mr. Longman looked about anxiously, for he was presented with a dilemma. If she were a lady, he could put her on his horse. But if anybody should see a female factory hand on his horse while he led her home, there would be tittering and gossip. But he quite liked Miss Coomb, she was comely and pert, so he gallantly offered his horse, which she accepted, and she allowed herself to be lifted up and seated side-saddle. Mr. Longman took the reins.

"You'll have to show me the way, Miss Coomb."

Debra undertook that part, and led the way. She was enthralled. Sally arriving home on Mr. Longman's horse! What would everybody in Crescent Court say? They turned onto Tithebarn Street towards

Byrum, where they knew a lot of people and hoped to be noticed.

"What a long way for you to walk to work and back," said Mr. Longman, a little anxious again. He saw passersby looking at them and smirking at the sight of Sally Coomb on a gentleman's horse. He glanced at his pocket watch.

"We're used to it," Sally said from her mount. "But we're very nearly there. Just a little way up Richmond Street, is our Court." Her heart thrilled at the thought of entering Crescent Court with Mr. Longman. He'd probably show her to the door! What would her stepmother say? She'd show her how well she could do for herself!

"I must leave you here," said Mr. Longman, to her disappointment, just before they came to the Court, while a little crowd of children, including Olivia and Julia, gathered round to watch the spectacle of the gentleman lifting Sally Coomb off the horse.

"Oh," she said. "Well, that's all right. I can lean on Debbie the rest of the way, I suppose. It was most kind of you to give me help, Mr. Longman. I shall be indebted to you."

## CHAPTER SIX

1855

It was a dreary November Monday afternoon, and a settled rain all day made Crescent Court look dark and dirty. Olivia watched for the lamplighter, and as always, he came around the corner, set his ladder against one lamppost, climbed up and lit the lamp, then got down again. He repeated the process for the other lamppost, and then left. After that nothing was happening outside, except that as the day darkened, the wet Court now had gleaming walls and cobbles where the lamps shone on them.

A stray dog wandered in, sniffed around, lifted his leg against one of the posts and went off again; Mrs. Coleman came out her door with a basket and set off into Richmond Street, and Mr. Barnes went in his door.

Olivia felt bored, until she wondered if Sally or Debra had got anything new. It was a long time since she had looked to see. She stole up the stairs, for she was banned from their room, and there was no end of trouble when they found their things moved.

The girls' room was small and cramped with a bed, a wardrobe, a chest of drawers and a chair somehow rammed inside, but they had made it look nice, with flowery wallpaper and prints on the walls, and a framed mirror hanging from a nail.

Olivia picked up the hairbrush with the pearly handle bought from a stall in Paddy's Market, and brushed her long dark hair. Bored with that, she opened a drawer and took out a fan, pirouetted about with it, then laying it to one side, she dived underneath the bed.

She scrambled out when she heard Julia's voice below on the street, calling her. She put her head out the window.

"I'm up here! Knock and Mama will let you in!"

Soon Julia's footsteps were on the stairs, and Olivia could hear her mother's voice calling her.

"Olivia! I hope you're not disturbing any of Sally's or Debra's things!"

"No, Mama!"

"Go into your own room and play, then!"

This was the room Olivia shared with her mother and brothers. She knew everything that was there, and novelty was not to be found in it. So she beckoned cautiously to her friend to come into the girls' room.

"I'm just going to look under the bed, that's where Sally keeps her secret things." she whispered.

Julia's eyes were round. "Big girls always have secrets," she complained. "Deirdre won't let me go near her box.

What's in under the bed?" she asked as all she could see of Livvy now were her two feet sticking out from it.

"Oh she pushed this back so far, it must be something very secret!" Olivia's voice was muffled as she wriggled her way out, with an enchanting pink and grey hatbox hugged to her chest.

"This is new!"

They sat on the floor and opened it, and parted the tissue wrapping to find a dainty hat in purple velvet, trimmed with red ribbon. Livvy took it out carefully.

"It's the most beautiful thing I ever saw in my life!" exclaimed Julia. "Deirdre has nothing like that! Where'd she get it? Look at the bows, and the feathers! Oh, I'd love a hat like that, I would!"

Livvy set it upon Julia's head.

"Let's play Princesses!" she said.

"But princesses wear crowns!"

"Not all the time. But we need more than a hat. Wait —" Livvy dived under the bed again, this time emerging with a wooden box, and opened it.

"Golly!" was Julia's response to the dazzling array of jewellery inside. "Can I touch this?" her finger extended timidly to a bracelet with pearly stones.

Livvy gave her permission, and their game began in earnest. A string of beads went around Julia's neck, the fan was picked up again, and Livvy wore the hat. They raided the drawers for Sunday shawls. Julia placed the pearly bracelet upon her head.

"I'll be Princess Louise and you can be Princess Alice," said Olivia. *"Where is our Mother, the Queen, today, Alice?"*

*"She's in the kitchen, cooking supper."*

"No, Julia, she isn't. Queens don't cook suppers! Say 'She's out in her carriage!'"

*"She's out in her carriage, dear."*

*"And where is our father, Alice dear?"*

*"Papa is out in Prince Menshikoff's carriage."*

"Who is Prince Menchikoff?" asked Olivia, her role set aside for the moment.

"I don't know, but Papa read about his carriage in the paper."

The bracelet on Julia's head began to slide off.

"Bend your head," Livvy said, reaching out and trying to widen the bracelet a little with her hands. She pulled—and a shower of white beads flew past their faces and rolled around the floor.

"Oh golly-gosh." Livvy said.

"Your sister will murder you!" was the comforting reply.

The girls wondered what to do, but there seemed to be little retrieval, except to find as many beads as they could and hide them away in the back of the wardrobe. They did not feel like playing Princesses anymore, so they pushed the boxes back in under the bed and slid down the banisters to the living room. Julia went home, wisely.

# CHAPTER SEVEN

Livvy dearly wanted to tell her mother about Sally's beautiful new hat, but she knew that disclosing it would lead to the discovery of her disobedience. There was only a temporary reprieve from retribution, however, after her stepsisters arrived home and went upstairs.

Angry shouts, louder and angrier, and Sally's boots thundering down the wooden stairs, calling for Olivia and Mother together.

Her stepmother came from the kitchen with a dishrag in her hand and stood at the foot of the stairs. Sally shrieked and pointed to Olivia.

"She's been into my room again! I thought you told her not to! It's a complete mess!"

"Olivia!" Mama turned to the offender, who was sitting innocently on the hearthrug. "Did you go in there after I told you not to?"

Olivia nodded her culpability.

"It's not just the mess in the room, I found this on the floor—one of the pearls from my good bracelet!" Sally sped downstairs to show Mrs. Coomb, holding the bead in the palm of her hand.

"Did you break your sister's bracelet, Olivia?" asked her mother sternly. Another nod.

"My pearls!" raged Sally. "The only decent piece of jewellery I have!"

"Well they aren't *real* pearls, Sally. Be reasonable. Though it was very wrong of Olivia to break them, and she will be punished."

"Oh *yes*, they *are* real pearls, they *are* indeed!"

"Don't be ridiculous! Where would you get real pearls? You can't afford real pearls!"

Sally seemed to think for a moment; then she stiffened and said,

"No matter. She broke my bracelet. She should be whipped."

Olivia was guilty, there was no way out of it. But her mother's reaction to Sally's having *real pearls* had not escaped her. She was not supposed to have them. Maybe, she was not supposed to have the hat either. Livvy found a way to turn the attention from herself to Sally.

"Sally has a new hat and it's a secret." she pronounced, with all the satisfaction of a prosecutor producing the evidence that would condemn the unfortunate in the dock. Her tactic worked a treat. All of her mother's attention was directed to Sally, as she demanded it to be produced.

Sally at first denied it, but the damage was done. Debra, now downstairs again, was glaring at Olivia.

"My fan, that Grandmamma gave me, has been thrown about like an old rag."

But nobody was listening. The hat was eventually fetched and argued about.

"I bought it with my own money!" Sally was protesting.

"That's impossible! You couldn't afford as good a hat as that! They don't even sell them that good anywhere we go! Who gave it you?"

"If you must know, my young man gave it to me."

"Your young man! Why haven't you mentioned that you 'ave a young man? It's not a crime. He must 'ave a good job. It's—it's not that *Longman*, I hope! Your father warned you off of him more than once!"

Sally's chin went up.

"It's Mr. Riley."

"Who is Mr. Riley?"

"The brother of Miss Mildred Riley I work with."

Maureen turned to Debra.

"Is that true?" she demanded.

Debra, without as much as a glance at Sally, nodded.

"What does Mr. Riley do for a living, that he can afford to give you expensive gifts like this?"

"He's a salesman."

"What does he sell?"

Sally paused.

"Jewellery."

"Well, Sally, I want to meet Mr. Riley, I do."

"That's impossible! He travels a lot and won't be back in Liverpool for a few weeks."

The argument continued over supper, Sally and Debra versus their stepmother. It was an ugly quarrel. At last Sally retorted that she wasn't her mother, which was the weapon both girls always used to drive the nail home and cause Mrs. Coomb to become morose and withdrawn and not speak to them for a few days.

Olivia sat through it. Everybody had forgotten her part in it, and she had escaped punishment. For a reason she did not understand, having a hat or a pearl bracelet given to you by a man was a lot more serious than disobeying your mother and playing with your sister's things. The row was unpleasant though; it made her unhappy to see everybody fighting, and that was her fault.

# CHAPTER EIGHT

1 856

Olivia and Julia loved fine Sundays when the days were becoming longer, because after the dinner wash-up was done, everybody went out in the country for a walk. The Sullivans often joined the Coombs and they made a large and very merry party. The older Sullivan girls were friends with Sally and Debra.

Uncle Jimmy often came as well. He regaled the younger children with stories. Olivia was very proud of him, because he had a fount of knowledge about the world. The children asked for the same stories over and over.

"All the O'Briens are cousins of the Earl of Rineanna. He lives in a castle called Dromosea, on the banks of the River Shannon."

"Why don't we go and visit him someday, Uncle Jimmy?"

"Why, we will. He's written many times to invite me, you know, but we have to wait awhile yet, because he's very busy catching poachers."

"Did he give you the snuff-box, Uncle Jimmy?"

"Yes, he had got it from a friend, but he had one already, so he gave it to me."

"Will you show it to us, Uncle Jimmy?"

"Of course, but not here, when we get home. It's in my pocket."

They had seen it many times, but always liked to see it again, for it was a beautiful object.

The truth about Uncle Jimmy's snuff box was that he had found it on a riverbank. It was made of ivory. He recognised it as one that had belonged to a gentleman. It bore a hunting scene on the lid, and an inscription on the back, in decorative writing. *"Patrick A. Fitzgerald, 21 years 1701"*

The mothers smiled to each other. Uncle Jimmy was never stuck for an answer to any question posed by his extravagant claims. But it was just a story for the children; with the adults he was perfectly sensible. He held the children in thrall, painted fantastic pictures for them with his descriptions of where he had allegedly been and the people he had met, and it seemed to them that he was a sort of mythical figure, himself.

One Sunday, while the small children were following Uncle Jimmy as if he were the Pied Piper of Hamelin, and the older ones had gone ahead, Mrs. Sullivan hung back a little, an uneasiness in her manner.

"I have to talk to you about an important matter," she began. "And I don't quite know how to broach it."

"Don't be afraid—it can't be too bad now, can it?"

"It's about your Sally."

"Sally?" Maureen pursed her lips. Sally, now eighteen, was still living at home, and there wasn't a beau in sight. After the quarrel about the hat, 'Mr. Riley' had apparently done a bunk. At any rate, Sally had never brought him to the door. She had not heard of anybody else, and Maureen had eased up on her questions as she had become older. She'd do herself up very nicely on Saturday nights, and on Sunday afternoons, when of late she had been declining to come on walks with the rest of the family. She was going to walk with her friends, she said.

"Do you know where she is today?"

"She's gone to the Farrells, she told me."

"Well, she's not gone to the Farrells. She's been keeping company with Mr. Longman from the Factory."

Maureen stopped dead.

"That can't be!" she said. "She promised her father! We thought she had stopped walking out with that fellow. Her father gave her a good lecture. He said that his like would never marry the daughter of a Packet Rat like him, and he forbade her to see him. And she promised 'im!"

"She might have kept to 'er word for a while, Maureen, but she's gone and broke it. And—"

"What is it, Mrs. Sullivan?"

"They have been seen getting out of a cab and going into a Hotel on Vauxhall Road. Tongues are wagging, Maureen."

"I'll say they are! How dare she lie to me! I wonder if Debra knows anything about this. I'll bet she does!"

"

Calm yourself, Maureen. You don't want her to leave your house, as long as she's coming back nights—"

"Is he serious about her, do you think? Might it be possible, Mrs. Sullivan, that he intends to marry 'er? If anything has 'appened, he will be made to marry her, for 'er father will make sure of it. I wish he'd get a shore job. I do. Those girls are too much for me."

There was a burst of merriment from the children surrounding Uncle Jimmy. The talk had moved on to Turkey, where he had been a guest of the Sultan, and sailed his yacht across the Bosporus, and fished, and caught a trout made of gold and silver, who begged to be put back, and so Uncle Jimmy put him back, and after that he had the greatest luck to catch the biggest fish in the Bosporus, and the Sultan gave him a gold ring.

"Where is it, Uncle Jimmy? The ring?"

"Why, I put it in the Bank of England for safekeeping," said their uncle.

"Hans Christian Andersen has nothing on him," remarked Mrs. Sullivan.

"I know. I'll get Jimmy to talk to her," said Maureen, her mind on more serious matters. "He's more of a father to them than their own."

# CHAPTER NINE

O livia was playing quietly on the hearthrug with her little brother Willie when she heard loud voices coming from the kitchen. She jumped to her feet in astonishment. Uncle Jimmy was cross! She ran to the door and opened it a crack to peep in.

"And so you are never to see that rake again, Sally. He means no good if he hasn't proposed marriage!"

"He loves me!" Sally shouted back.

"If he loved you, he wouldn't be taking you to hotels!" she heard her mother say. "You've been seen; the whole town is talking about you!"

"Don't let him ruin you, Sally. I've a mind to go and tell your grandfather and get him to go and see this rake. I know his type—" Uncle Jimmy stopped abruptly and thumped the table. The table legs shuddered under the assault and the crockery wobbled.

"Oh no, don't go and see Grandfather!" said Sally, quite horrified.

"I just might go and see the fellow myself," said Uncle Jimmy, quite in a rage now.

"Don't, Jimmy. Bertie is due back on Tuesday. He'll go."

"What's the delay in giving you the ring?" demanded Uncle Jimmy. Olivia had never heard him so angry in her life!

Olivia didn't want to hear any more. She ran out of the house and opened the front door of number 6.

"Please can Julia come out to play," she asked tearfully.

Julia extracted herself from under the table where she'd taken her abacus. Together they walked down the street and Olivia told her what had happened.

"I never saw Uncle Jimmy cross before!"

"But he wasn't cross with you, so it doesn't matter. And Sally is a bad girl."

"Is she? A bad girl?"

"My father said so. He said that if he was her father, he'd lay a whip around her."

"Is she as bad as all that?" Olivia was incredulous.

"She must be," Julia answered. "Livvy, let's go to Mary Fisher's house and play hopscotch."

Olivia was happy to oblige and she forgot all about Sally being a bad girl and Uncle Jimmy's raised voice.

When she returned, all was calm.

"Why was Uncle Jimmy so cross?" she asked her mother.

"Because he's worried about Sally. That she'll ruin herself."

"How?"

But her mother did not answer.

The following morning, after Olivia got up, her mother was upset. Sally was gone, and with her went her best clothes and shoes. Debra claimed to be as surprised as anybody else and said she had slept well all night and not heard her leaving.

Mr. Coomb was expected back the next day.

# CHAPTER TEN

**M**aureen wanted to meet her husband at the landing stage, rather than allow Debra, who had stayed at home from work, to impart the bad news. She wrapped herself up in her shawl and walked down to where the *Adonis* was to be berthed. She saw it on the horizon and watched it get larger and larger. She became apprehensive. What would Bertie say? Would he blame her for being negligent?

The rope was thrown in, the ship tied up, the passengers disembarked, the mail taken off, and now it was the crew's turn. She watched as sailor after sailor came down the gangway, scanning for her husband's face. Sometimes he was late, if there was some complication with a boiler, but she spotted another boilerman, Mr. Cutler, coming ashore, and waved to him.

He saw her and it seemed to her that he advanced reluctantly toward her, his head down.

"Mr. Cutler! Where's Mr. Coomb? Is he delayed?"

"Delayed?" said Mr. Cutler. "He never came to the ship! And we missed him, we did, because there were only the few of us, and it's 'ard work, as you know, Mrs. Coomb."

"Why didn't he come to the ship? Is he ill?"

"Not that I've 'eard, Mrs. Coomb. I'm sorry, I don't know any more than that," he rearranged his pack on his shoulder and passed on. In the meantime, the other boilermen had passed by, out of the corner of her eye she saw them, glancing at her and was it her imagination that they hastened their steps to pass?

"Where's Captain Peabody?"

"He's on his way." Mr. Cutler went on his way.

Maureen, very worried now, shifted from foot to foot until she saw an officer disembark—the First Mate, Mr. Golding. Captain Peabody was a little way behind him, a crewman carrying his trunk.

"Excuse me, Captain Peabody—" Maureen was shaking with nerves now. "I'm Mrs. Coomb, wife to your boilerman Albert Coomb, can you tell me what's happened to my 'us and why 'e wasn't on the ship?"

The Captain halted and bowed his head a little.

"Mrs. Coomb, I'm afraid I am quite at a loss as to the whereabouts of your husband. All I know is that he failed to report for duty upon our return voyage from New York."

"Did you telegraph your New York Office?" said Mrs. Coomb, very agitated now. "Perhaps he just missed the sailing through an accident, or something like!"

She noticed that the Captain avoided her eyes.

"You know!" she accused him. "Did you sack him, was that it?"

"You are mistaken, Madam, I did not. We reached New York, and he disappeared, and when I questioned the men, they did not know where he had gone, but I think, if you would do a little more probing from Mr. Cutler or Mr. Boyle, they might be able to help you more than I. Good day, Madam. I am sorry not to be of more help to you." He tipped his hat and went upon his way, signalling to his crewman to take up the trunk again, which he had laid down.

Maureen rushed home in distress, pulling her shawl around her. What was wrong? Where did Cutler and Boyle live?

Unknown to her, Olivia had followed her down to the landing stage instead of staying with the servant, Susan, and witnessed the entire episode. Now she followed her home again, catching up with her and crying. Maureen caught her hand and tried to reassure her, but her heart was not in it. Something dreadful had happened to Bertie, something so truly dreadful that they could not bear to tell her. He wasn't dead—they'd have told her that. Or ill—there is no shame in illness. They knew something, because they had not put forward any theories.

What was it?

# CHAPTER ELEVEN

Olivia and Maureen had been home about an hour when a knock came to the door. Maureen was relieved to see Mr. Cutler and Mr. Boyle standing there, even if their weather-beaten, red faces showed no joy.

"Take John and go into the kitchen, Olivia," Maureen said. Olivia reluctantly obeyed. But once inside, she put her ear to the door.

"Tell me the truth." She heard her mother say.

"It's like this, Mrs. Coomb. Your 'usband was involved in some funny business over the last few years, and, well—'e's been caught."

"Funny business! What kind of funny business? Caught!"

Olivia frowned. John began to talk but she shushed him.

"He wor gambling, and mixin' with unsavoury types, and 'e wor in a fight, and it got very serious, a man ended up getting killed, and Bertie was arrested—for murder."

"You're not serious."

"We are. He's in prison in New York, awaiting trial."

Then followed a cry, and chair legs scraping, and some odd sounds, and "Mrs. Coomb! Jack, call for 'elp. Get a neighbour, Jack! Go next door."

Olivia could bear it no longer, she rushed out to the living room to see her mother lying on the floor, her lips and face whitened like chalk.

"Mama!" she cried, and was joined by John, and William, who woke from his nap.

The rest of the day was the worst she had ever seen in her life. Deirdre Sullivan came in and looked after her and the boys, and Mrs. Sullivan made endless cups of tea for her mother, who seemed to be unable to do anything at all except sit by the fire and weep, asking "why?"

Debra came home from work and like her stepmother, became weak and ill at the news. Deirdre Sullivan made supper for everybody.

Olivia's grandparents had been summoned and came in later, and Mrs. Sullivan and Deirdre left. Everybody had questions to which nobody had answers. What were the prisons like in America? Would he be allowed a defence? What sort of judge could he expect? Would an Englishman get a fair trial? And where was the money to come from to employ lawyers and barristers? Or had he been tried already, and found guilty? Or was he out of jail and hurrying across to them even as they spoke? There were no answers, and a morbid silence enveloped the room as darkness fell.

"Where's Sally?" asked old Mrs. Coomb suddenly.

And then it came out that Sally had absconded two days before. Mr and Mrs. Coomb were very angry that they had been left in the dark for two full days, and their daughter-in-law's pleas that her father had a right to know first, and to take the first action, fell on deaf ears.

Olivia knew that everything had changed. She felt a burden on her heart, it made her feel very sad, very frightened.

She longed to see Uncle Jimmy—why wouldn't he come? He would make everything all right. He would! She had so much to ask him! What was *gambling*? And what was *'charged with murder'*? There were other big words she did not remember, but those seemed to carry the most trouble.

# CHAPTER TWELVE

M r. and Mrs. Coomb walked back to their home in darkness, their hearts full of heaviness and not a little anger.

"I'm sure this is a set-up," Mr. Coomb said. "Albert is a good boy, he never done anything wrong."

"All he did wrong was to marry that Maureen O'Brien," said his wife.

"We can't blame her for his present trouble, though."

"Maybe not, but are we to look after her now, and the family? And not to tell us that Sally was gone, eloped! There was some great neglect there. She was allowed to run wild. I don't blame Sally. Bertie should have chosen a better woman for his motherless children."

"Never mind Sally for now. It's Bertie. Up for murder! Doris, I'm going over to America."

They reached their house, and Alfred put his key in the lock. He lit a lamp and the living-room gained a soft, shadowy light. There were sounds of fighting from upstairs—the Mooneys were at it again, they were always either singing or fighting.

"I have to make plans, quickly. I have to leave in the next few days, Doris."

"I'm coming with you, Alf."

"No, you better stay and look after Maureen—"

"I'm coming with you, Alf. I will be there with my son! What kind of place is America, that would do this to an innocent man? I won't rest until I see him free!"

"We need money, so we'll put the house up for sale at the soonest, Doris."

"She'll have to move, then!" This was said with a little spite and triumph.

"We'll get a quick sale and be off. What'll we do with this flat?"

"What do you mean, what will we do? You're not thinking they'll move in here, are you? Because I won't have her using my pots and pans and the crockery, everything would be abused and broken in no time at all. Those children of hers are out of control."

"What will we do with our things, then?"

"Sell them, Alf. Nothing is as important as our Bertie, and I don't give a straw for anything I have. Engage that fellow your friend Perrot knows—the attorney Lawson. He'll arrange a loan for us, and we can be off directly. Then 'e can sell the 'ouse and furniture to repay the loan."

"And this flat, Doris?"

"The attorney can include the furniture in the sale."

Alf took the lamp into the bedroom as Doris followed.

"It doesn't seem fair to leave Maureen with nothing," he said. "And her children are our grandchildren. Doris, you said that you didn't give a straw about your things, and yet you won't leave them for her to use!"

"Are you trying to start a fight, Alf? Because if you are, I'll let you 'ave a fight. Our son Bertie is in grave need and all you can think of is that stupid woman he married! What do we care for Maureen O'Brien! I wish 'e had never set eyes on her! Roberta was the perfect woman for him."

"I wasn't—I didn't—"

"Our only child, Albert John is about to be hanged for murder! Do they hang people in America, or shoot them? Or chop off their 'eads? How do we know anything about what it's like for him over there, in a strange country, in prison with Americans, do they even speak English? He is deprived of every comfort, 'as no visitors, and is at the mercy of foreigners!" She sank onto the bed and burst into tears.

"We'll sell everything," he said hastily. "And—why don't we take Debra too?" He was thinking that the company of his wife would be very taxing, and that to have another female would help him greatly as Debra could be useful at these times, and if the worse came to the worst—he did not want to think about that.

"Roberta's daughter!" Mrs. Coomb looked up and wiped her eyes on the corner of her shawl. "Oh yes, Debra would be a great comfort! We'll take Debra with us!"

"I will go to Mr. Perrot first thing tomorrow. I don't know if my job will be kept for me, but when we come back, *with Bertie*, we can cross that bridge. Will you tell Maureen?"

"Yes, I'd like that."

The old couple got into bed, and Alf turned down the lamp. Sleep would come to neither.

"Alfred?"

Alf knew that a great thought was germinating in his wife's mind.

"Alfred?" this a little impatiently, just after the first.

"Might we never come back to England, if, say, Bertie is in prison for a very long time?"

Alf sat up immediately.

"What are you saying, wife?"

She sat up also.

"I'm saying, that if it goes wrong for Bertie, and 'e gets convicted of manslaughter, not murder, he won't be 'anged perhaps, but he might be years and years in prison. If he does, I'm not coming back."

"I see," he mulled after a few moments.

"How could we, Alf, come back without Bertie?"

"We couldn't."

"So—you see."

There was more to be discussed, their plans enlarged, and they talked for another hour.

# CHAPTER THIRTEEN

**M**r. Edward Slater read the letter again. It was from Henry, and its contents astonished and aggravated him. He read it aloud to his wife.

*Dear Aunt and Uncle, I am truly sorry, but something very unexpected and important has come up, and I have to leave you without saying goodbye. I appreciate greatly all you have done for me in the past two years, in opening your home and your business to me. I consider myself ready to set up on my own, but as we agreed, not in Liverpool. However—that is not of course the reason for my sudden departure. I have been summoned to an emergency, but pray do not worry, it does not concern any illness in the family. Circumstances are such that I cannot disclose any more. In haste, therefore, your esteemed nephew, Henry.*

"Something happened, Edward."

"But what can have happened to make him leave so abruptly? I'm at a complete loss."

"Though he is my sister's child, Edward, I say that Henry Longman is no loss."

Mr. and Mrs. Slater lived at Knotty Ash in a large Georgian mansion with a small but tastefully laid out park. Mrs. Slater was a delicate-looking, silent woman—on first acquaintance she seemed even mousey, but those who tried to take advantage of her underestimated her. She spoke little, but she was cunning. Her one aim in life was to become rich. She had always envied those richer than her, and was acutely conscious of her own humble origins, so she never spoke of them.

The Slaters' marriage was built on the premise that they would become very wealthy. Their backgrounds were similar; both fathers, neighbours from the Vauxhall area, had enlisted together in the Navy as young men during the Peninsular Wars. Sargent Slater was a cook on *the Alice*, and Sargent Colly was batman to her Captain. Captain Armstrong thought highly of his batman and after the War, upon hearing that Colly wished to start a business, he lent him Prize money on very generous terms.

Colly and Slater went into business as confectioners. They rented premises at Old Hall Street. Slater made sweets and chocolates, Colly ably managed the business end. Each married, and their children were friends.

At fourteen years old, Edward Slater and Jemima Colly discovered a common aim in life—both wanted, more than anything else, to become rich. The parents saw and encouraged the attachment, for they were in business together, but Mr. and Mrs. Slater, gentle, generous people, did not share the worldly ambitions of the Collys. They saw avarice in them. Mr. Colly had pestered Mr. Slater for years to add a little *taft* to the sweets; the supposedly harmless ingredient made of plaster of Paris and limestone. Slater resisted—a true craftsman did not use false ingredients! They had customers because of the quality of their product—people trusted them! How could they break their trust?

Mr. and Mrs. Slater were very disappointed that their son Edward also tried to persuade his father to adulterate the sweets, and relations between the two families became strained, but the engagement of

Edward and Jemima set it back upon a better footing. There was no adulteration, and Mr. Colly never asked again.

Edward's marriage to Jemima was happy. He also was very keen to get ahead, he had his eye on a seat in parliament, perhaps. Other businessmen had risen to take their places among England's bejewelled stars. Money was beginning to matter as much nowadays as Lineage. They discussed it all the time at night, when she was sewing and he was reading out snippets from the newspaper about other families in Liverpool who were worthy of mention by dint of a prestigious appointment or a marriage.

A son, Franklin, was born to them. Jemima, too busy and involved in the factory, sent him and his nurse to Edward's parents for long intervals. Old Mrs. Slater was only too happy to have her grandson, and to guide him as best she could away from the avaricious nature of both parents.

Chandelier Chocolates was thriving, they had expanded and now employed fifty people. Edward, who alone ran the business now as the Collys had no son, began to adulterate the sweets, and nobody was any the wiser.

A few years before, Jemima's sister, Mrs. Longman, had written from Norfolk asking if she could send her son Henry to them to learn the confectionery business. They were gratified—for Paulina had married into a gentleman's family, though the Longmans hardly had two pennies to rub together, due to a fortune lost in Monte Carlo by Henry's father. It made them feel important that they could assist the son of a real gentleman. They had agreed, on condition that when he was ready to start out on his own, that he would not set up in Liverpool.

Henry came to them and they endured rather than enjoyed his company. He was not energetic and dashing as a young gentleman ought to be, but had a lethargy and dullness with little to say for himself. Now who would have thought that he could just disappear, out of the blue, without saying anything at all? What dreadful ingratitude!

They heard the knock on the front door—who could it be, at this time of night? Surely not Henry? If so, he was on foot—no cab was heard.

"Mason's locked up for the night—I shall go down," Mr. Slater said, rising. Jemima, curious, followed him.

He opened the door. A young woman stood there in the darkness. Astonished, they heard what she had to say. Then it all became clear.

"We're engaged, we are. I went to the place where we were to meet, and 'e wasn't there. What's 'appened to him?"

"He's gone away." Mrs. Slater pursed her lips.

"Gone away, where?"

"He left Liverpool." Mrs. Slater insisted.

"But where did 'e go?" pleaded the girl.

"He didn't say. He left us a note to say he had to leave Liverpool. For good." Mr. Slater expanded. "Your voice is familiar," he added with suspicion. "Who are you? Do you work for us?"

The girl seemed to freeze upon the doorstep, then turned on her heel and left, running down the avenue. Mr. Slater shut the door.

"She works for us—I know she does. But as to her name, and what room, I don't know. But it is all clear now, Mrs. Slater, is it not?"

"Good riddance to bad rubbish," said his wife. "If you find out who she is, get rid of her immediately. As for Henry, as I said, we're well rid of him. All that money we spent on him, all those dinners we gave for him, and he sets up with a hussy like that."

"I hope she's not—not—" began Mr. Slater nervously.

"What if she is? It's nothing to do with us. He's only a nephew. Forget them both."

# CHAPTER FOURTEEN

When Mr. Slater went to the factory the following morning, he called the foreman and asked him if everybody was present.

"No, sir. There's two hands from Sugaring out, and one from Roasting, that's two days she's missed."

"Are they men or women?"

"The two from Sugaring are men, then there's Miss Coomb from Roasting."

"Two days. Any word from her?"

"Her sister works 'ere too, and she says she's sick."

"Her sister, eh? I want to walk through the room, Jenkins, and just point her out to me."

"Very well, sir"" They went upstairs and entered the Roasting room, the heat blasting both in their faces, and Jenkins indicated a girl who was shuffling a pan of coffee beans before tipping them into the roaster. They walked on.

"I want you to let her go, Jenkins."

"Sir? She's a good worker."

"That is of no concern. She's to go this evening."

Jenkins swallowed.

"May I enquire as to why, sir?"

"You may not."

There was a pause.

"Is Mr. Henry coming back, sir?"

"What interest do you have in Mr. Longman's affairs, Jenkins?"

"Oh, no interest at all, sir. I just wondered."

"You may stop wondering. It's none of your business. Do you understand?"

"Yes, sir."

"And—I do not want to hear that there is any gossip about Mr. Longman, Jenkins. If it comes to my ears, you're dismissed."

Mr. Jenkins swallowed again and nodded. Everybody knew about Miss Coomb and Mr. Longman. He'd have to give all a stern warning not to speak of it. But an elopement—if that is what it was—between a hand and the owner's nephew would make for a great deal of talk, especially for the women.

Debra had seen Mr. Jenkins nod his head toward her and though she did not acknowledge either man, saw too that Mr. Slater stared at her.

It was about Sally of course. They knew about her and Mr. Longman. Where was Sally? Where was Mr. Longman? Both gone. Eloped, most likely, to Gretna Green. It was well for them! Those in Crescent Court were in great turmoil, with Papa in prison in New York.

They'd need every penny now. She wondered if she could do extra hours.

Mr. Jenkins called her name as she was putting on her bonnet and gave her her wages and told her she was dismissed, no reason.

She was stunned and walked back to Crescent Court feeling very ill.

CHAPTER FIFTEEN

Sally's fate was the least of Maureen's worries. Everybody assumed that she and Mr. Longman had eloped and that they must have settled somewhere in the North of England, and having decided it that way, put Sally out of their heads for now.

Mrs. Coomb came in the morning.

"Alfred and I are leaving directly for New York," she said bluntly. "And we're selling this house to pay for Bertie's defence."

. . .

"I was thinking the same thing," Maureen said eagerly. "In fact, why do we all not go to New York? My place is with my husband in his time of need."

Olivia was standing beside her, trying to understand.

*New York! That's where Papa was and if they all went there, everything would be all right.*

This is not what Mrs. Coomb expected to hear. She was convinced that Maureen did not love Bertie, and it made her cross, rather than glad, to hear that she cared for her husband and was prepared to make the sacrifice.

"We can't afford it," she said stiffly. "We will leave, and then send for you. Mr. Coomb will find work there."

Maureen looked at her with doubt.

"We're selling everything we 'ave," Mrs. Coomb went on. "Including everything in this house."

.  .  .

This was quite a bit harder to take.

"I do have Bertie's children to look after," Maureen said, knowing that she was of little or no consequence to the Coomb family. She pulled Olivia close.

"Your children need their father more than they need luxuries." snapped Mrs. Coomb.

"Furniture is not luxury. Bertie wouldn't want you to leave us with nothing at all."

"And another thing—we're taking Debra with us."

Maureen caught her breath. Debra was now the only wage-earner in the house.

"Debra," she repeated.

.  .  .

"Mr. Coomb is at this moment seeing an attorney, and tomorrow, there will be men here to pack everything up and put it in auction rooms. You'll have to find yourself some accommodation, for we are to move out of our flat tomorrow, and will stay in lodgings until we board, which hopefully will be the day after. Pack up Debra's clothes and send 'er to us in the morning."

"But where—can it not be done another way, Mrs. Coomb?" Maureen exclaimed, and Olivia felt herself pressed to her mother's side as she laid a protective arm over her. The boys were playing some invented game of their own and were not taking any notice. "Allow us to take your flat! I'll work—"

"It has been decided. You 'ave your brother to help you, don't you? And your cousin in London? Now there is no more time to discuss this; Bertie's hungry and cold. and we should not even think of our own comfort, or inconvenience, or how 'ard we have it. I must leave you—send Debra! And another thing—" she hesitated.

. . .

"What?"

"We will take the boys with us, and you follow afterwards with Olivia."

"Oh no," Maureen exclaimed. "You won't. That's out of the question. Our family is not going to be split up."

It was the most decisive statement Maureen had ever made to her mother-in-law.

"You won't be able to feed them. Let us 'ave them, and we'll see they want for nothing."

"No. They're staying with me. My brother and my cousin will 'elp me. You've said it yourself."

. . .

Maureen's voice was unusually firm, though there was a little tremor. The idea of being separated from her children was more than she could bear.

Olivia was very, very relieved that her grandmother did not suggest *she* go with them to America. But she took it into her head that they might, yet. She would not rest easy until they had gone.

CHAPTER SIXTEEN

Olivia's mother told her to go and fetch Mrs. Sullivan, and to her she poured out all the latest developments. Olivia understood it more clearly now. She kept by her mother's side, afraid, until Mrs. Sullivan told her to go and play with Julia. But her play was mechanical, and Julia told her brightly that everything would be all right, could they not go and live with Uncle Jimmy? Olivia brightened up, there was nothing she would like better! Uncle Jimmy came that very evening and gave her mother money—no, they were not to move in with him, but he had found her a few rooms in Daffodil Court, Scotland Road. It wasn't much—Uncle Jimmy did not have much.

"But he has a gold ring in the Bank of England!" cried Olivia.

"No, child—he was telling you a Tall Tale."

"What's a Tall Tale?"

"A fairy story to amuse you."

The truth did not amuse Olivia, and she felt a little resentful.

"Is he related to the Earl of—of Rineanna?"

"No, little lamb, if we were related to the Earl of Rineanna, we wouldn't be here. We'd be living in a castle."

So their world was just this—no castle, no gold ring. And Uncle Jimmy had stopped being happy. He had a grim, serious look that she hadn't seen before, as he helped her mother to pack.

When Debra came in later, with the story of her dismissal, she was delighted to hear that her future would be taken care of—New York sounded like so glamorous a place, so new and exciting—and she would be near her father. They could all come home together in a few months and then she'd go and live with Sally as she had always planned. It was to be her reward for keeping silent about her romance with Mr. Longman and telling lies for her.

She packed her clothes with a light heart, and feeling suddenly sorry for Olivia, that she was not having the same treat, so she gave her her fan.

# CHAPTER SEVENTEEN

Scotland Road had a noisy, but spirited air. Its inhabitants and those of nearby courts and streets frequented its myriad shops and quite as many pubs. Traffic rumbled up and down, the shrill cries of costermongers rose above the din; furtive footpads crept up behind unsuspecting victims, policemen on their beat were alert.

Daffodil Court was squeezed between Scottie Road and the street behind it, crammed with old, dilapidated terraced houses, most of which were divided into tiny flats, with crumbling outside staircases giving access to the upper floors.

Their new home was on the ground floor—one dingy room with a large fireplace, cracks in the walls and bare stone flags. Uncle Jimmy did the best he could to furnish it with two beds, a few chairs and rugs, and he brought in a sack of coal and made a fire.

"I'm sorry it's not better," he said.

It troubled Maureen that she was not to go to America, but she did not have the fare, and unless her children were to come also, it was out of the question.

She needed to work, though, and she also needed to make an arrangement for the children while she worked. But she did not have to do it just now, Jimmy had given her some money—all he had, she suspected.

The passage was booked for Friday, just a few days off, on the *Yorkman*. Debra had moved into the boarding house with her grandparents.

"Grandmama says can you come over to say goodbye?" she appeared in their new abode the day after they moved in, and looked around with distaste, thankful she would never have to live there. "They want to see the children."

"I'll bring them tomorrow morning," Maureen said. She had a letter for them to give to Bertie. Deirdre Sullivan had written it for her. What a terrible thing it was not to be able to read or write! Her children would learn, by hook or by crook!

The following morning, Olivia learned that she was to go and say goodbye to her grandparents. She pouted, the uneasy feeling once more that her grandmother would order her to come with them. She twirled the ends of her long dark hair.

"I don't want to go, Mama."

"Why not, child?"

"She'll want me to go away, too!"

"No, she won't." This was said in such a definite tone of voice that Olivia was partly reassured. But she fidgeted the entire evening.

*That girl is so sensitive*, thought Maureen. *Why is she all nerves?*

The following day, Olivia washed her face and hands and dressed herself in her Sunday best, her mother put a bow in her hair and the family set off for the *Stella* boarding house in one of the numerous streets up from the docklands. The Coombs had a room on the first floor.

"Where's all your luggage?" asked Maureen, looking about and only seeing a few small personal bags about.

"They're gone to the ship," her father-in-law said.

"Already! But you're not sailing till tomorrow."

"We sent them down to a warehouse and they'll be put on board for us tomorrow morning. What would be the point of hauling them up here to these rooms?" He seemed agitated, nervous, anxious, she thought, to be off. This was a very worrisome time for all of them.

"Oh, I see." Maureen produced the letter.

"Don't forget this for Bertie."

He put it in his inner pocket and sat down, running his hands through his grey hair. They all felt troubled.

"Debra, pour the children some milk from the jug."

"Yes, Grandmama."

"Maureen, you'll join us in some tea." Mrs. Coomb went to the landing and shouted down for tea to be brought up. While her father-in-law engaged her in conversation, she poured Maureen a cup.

There was far too much sugar in it; Mrs. Coomb was very distracted with all the trouble, Maureen did not care either way about the sugar but as she drained it, she saw that Olivia, John and William were drowsy, their heads falling onto their shoulders. Too late, she knew, too, that there was something in her tea, and she fought it—but in vain. All went dark, and she had an overwhelming feeling that something very terrible was about to occur.

## CHAPTER EIGHTEEN

When Olivia awakened, she was lying in a strange bed, in an even stranger place, a long room crammed with white beds, with a person in each one—all children. Sunlight streamed in the long windows. She was wearing a long white nightgown, crinkly and stiff, and a cap.

*What day was it? What time was it? Where was she?*

"Mama! Mama!" she cried out.

. . .

The girl in the bed next to her, so near that she could have put her hand out to hold hers, was older than she, and said,

"Are you awake, then? I'm Jenny. What's your name?"

"Olivia. Why am I here?"

"Because you're poorly. That's why we're all here." Olivia could hear a baby cry somewhere.

A woman came walking down the ward and Olivia ducked under the blankets, for she wore a very odd headdress. She'd never seen anything like it.

"Is she awake now?" she asked as she squeezed herself in between the two beds. "Uncover your head, child, so I can see you. I have some medicine for you."

Olivia uncovered her head. The headdress was not so fearful close up. It was a veil with three corners. The lady's eyes were kind.

.   .   .

"Medicine! I'm not poorly! Why am I 'ere?"

"Because you went into a very deep sleep and we had to watch you."

"Where is this place? Where's Mama?"

"This is the Northern Hospital. Come on, open your mouth. There! That wasn't too bad, was it? Oh dear, what a face!"

The medicine tasted horrid. The nurse went away but came back a little while later with a ledger that she set upon a little table at the foot of the bed. She took a pencil from her pocket.

"Tell me about yourself, Olivia. Your name and age, and where you live. And who your mother and father are."

.   .   .

Olivia told her as best she could, but could not remember the place where they had just moved into.

"Where's my mother? Where's John and Willie?"

"Is Olivia going to be cured, Nurse Barrett?" asked Jenny.

"Yes. Now, come with me," the nurse said, holding out her hand. "Let me see how you can walk." She helped her out of bed. Olivia felt a little unsteady on her legs, but within a moment or two, all was well. The nurse wrapped a little shawl around her and they went out of the ward, into a hallway and up a stairs. When they reached the top, the nurse said,

"There are some very ill patients in this room, so don't make a sound."

She opened a door very quietly and Olivia followed. There were several beds with people sleeping in them, and nurses flitting about quietly.

.  .  .

"Tell us if you see your mother here," said Nurse Barrett.

She led her from bed to bed. Here, there was an old woman without teeth. Beside her, there was a young woman with dark hair and a bloodstained dressing on her face. Olivia shivered. Next, joy gripped her heart.

"Mama!" she whispered with urgency, running to the bedside. But her mother was asleep.

"Mama, please wake up!"

The nurses looked at each other. But they smiled when Maureen's eyes opened. Olivia threw herself on the delicate figure.

"Oh Mama! I woke up in this place—I didn't know where I was—I didn't know where you were!"

.  .  .

"Thank God you're safe! Where are John and Willie? What happened? The last thing I remember is drinking tea. I saw the children's heads droop. What happened?"

Olivia was upon the bed and in her mother's arms now as she posed these questions to the nurses.

"You were found unconscious in an alley near the docks," said a doctor, who had just joined them. "The police were called and brought you here."

"But my sons? My little boys? Where are *they?*"

"Boys? There were no boys. Just you and a little girl, lying in a doorway."

"No, no, my two sons. Oh no—oh no!" Mrs. Coomb jumped out of bed. "They've been kidnapped! What was the name of that lodging house—the *Stella—Stella*! Fetch the police! Please —now!"

Mrs. Coomb staggered and fell against the small table beside the bed. The nurses ran to her and made her get into bed again.

"Quick, quick—before *the Yorkman* sails for America —my boys will be put on board! There's no time to be lost! Hurry—I've a terrible feeling they're taking them from me for good, they are! Now I know their plan!"

"*The Yorkman* sailed last evening with the tide, Mrs. Coomb. I read it in the *Daily Post,*" said the doctor.

"Oh no—it can't be true! It can't! Oh, isn't there anything we can do to catch it? My boys are on that ship, kidnapped by their grandparents! I know they are!"

Olivia was aghast. She burst into sobs.

·  ·  ·

"What are we going to do, Mama?" she asked, after a moment, through her tears. "I don't want them to go to New York!"

"I'm very much afraid that it will be too late to do anything," said Nurse Barrett. "If they've been on the water for nearly twenty-four hours." She shook her head.

"I must leave now," begged Mrs. Coomb. "Doctor, discharge me please, now."

"You're not in condition to be released yet, Mrs. Coomb. You're in a very agitated state, and the effects of the drug haven't worn off. You're a danger to yourself. You must rest. And Olivia must return to her ward."

Nurse Barrett took her by the hand and she felt herself reluctantly led away. She glanced back at her mother, who was sobbing in a heartbroken way.

.   .   .

A stream of light coming in the window illuminated another face as she was led to the door. Olivia hung back for a better look, so that the nurse found her dragging her hand.

"Why do you look at that patient? Do you know her?"

"Yes, I think it's Sally."

"Sally? Sally who?"

The doctor came up then.

"Do you know her? What's her name?"

"She's Sally Coomb, my sister. She's married."

.   .   .

The nurses looked at each other.

"Your sister!"

Nurse Barrett let go of her hand so that she could go nearer.

"Yes, it's Sally orright."

"Her name is Sally Coomb, then?"

"How funny! We thought she was gone away with Mr. Longman."

"Come, let's go back to your ward now."

"But I want to tell Mama that Sally is here! Is Sally very poorly?"

.   .   .

"Yes, I'm afraid so. You see, she nearly drowned in the canal. But she was pulled out just in time."

Olivia allowed herself to be led away and back to her ward, where she climbed into bed.

"Did you find your mother?" whispered Jenny.

"Yes."

"Are you going 'ome tomorrow?"

"I don't know. Are you going 'ome?"

"No, and if I do, it will only be for a little while. I spend most of the time in here. I have diabetes."

"What's that?"

. . .

"It means I'm going to Heaven soon. I can't say I mind, because Jesus told me I'll be well again."

"When you go to Heaven, will you ask Jesus to send my brothers back from New York?" Olivia began to sob.

Nurse Barrett told her to go to sleep, so she slid under the blankets and cried silently.

## CHAPTER NINETEEN

Early the following morning, Olivia woke up and slipped out of the ward, ran down the hall and upstairs to her mother. She found her mother up and dressed. Her face was puffy and her eyes swollen with crying. Olivia hugged her.

"I was just coming to find you," her mother said. "We're going. We have to go to the police."

"Mrs. Coomb, before you go, can you identify this woman? Your daughter said last night that—"

a nurse began, nodding to Sally's bed where she still slept.

.  .  .

"Goodness! That's my stepdaughter! What's she doing here?"

The nurse repeated what she had told Olivia, only this time, she added that somebody had seen her go into the canal and raised the alarm.

"Poor Sally! She didn't marry, then! Poor foolish girl! I hope she isn't—?"

"She's not. We don't think so."

"We need her full name and address, and next-of-kin." The nurse was ready with her ledger.

"Sally Ann Coomb, of—oh dear, her mother's dead, and her house is gone. Her father's in America, and her grandparents are on the high seas—with my two little boys!" her voice caught, before she recollected herself. "You had better put down my address, for she has nowhere else. And I suppose I'm her next-of-kin too. Listing her father, as he's in America and likely to stay there some time, is no good at all."

"When she's ready to go home, she'll go to you, then."

Mrs. Coomb nodded.

Olivia made a face. She did not want Sally back! Her brothers of course, Debra *maybe*, but not Sally!

"Come on, let's go down to your ward and you can get dressed." Her mother said, when that was done. "We have a lot to do today."

# CHAPTER TWENTY

By now, Debra was very angry. They were out in the Atlantic surrounded by heaving, turbulent waters, the ship pitched and rolled; the boys were still crying for their mother and sea-sick with it. Their grandmother was ill, too, and kept to her bunk. It fell to Debra to look after the children and it was very hard, with many other people milling around in steerage, other passengers ill, the smell of sick everywhere and groaning and general mayhem.

It wasn't right, what her grandparents had done to Mother. She'd seen it all! How the children fell asleep, then Mother realising something was wrong, and trying to fight it, but no good, she fell back in the chair, insensible.

Then two men had come and carried Mother and Olivia away, and the landlady had wanted to know what was going on. She was told that they had typhoid, and so she had practically run the men out with their burdens.

Debra had been horrified. Where had they been taken to? Had they been murdered? When she realised that the boys were to go to America with them, she'd objected strongly.

"We're not taking them with us!" Debra had cried in protest. "Mother doesn't know—and she will be out of her mind!"

"We know what's best, Debra. Don't question us."

The boys had been carried by Grandmama and herself, and Grandpapa carried all the rest of their bags as they struggled down to the ship, moored at the quayside.

"Sleepyheads," said Grandmama to everybody who had remarked on the children. "They din't sleep a wink last night with the excitement, and now look at 'em!"

They boarded and proceeded to the very darkest and lowest part of the ship, or so it seemed to Debra.

They found their bunks—slats of wood—in the middle of the hold filled with other passengers, all trying to make a little corner of home for the voyage. Some people wore strange clothes and chattered in foreign languages. Small children cried; their fatigued and bewildered wailings seemed contagious, and after John and Willie woke up, they joined their strong, bewildered voices to the rest. The noise and the smells were unbearable.

Debra wanted to go up on deck to escape it all, but she was not allowed to show her face in public until they'd sailed. Her grandfather paced to and fro in a state of nerves, until the rope was cast off and the giant hull heaved itself away from the wall.

"What happened to Mother and Olivia?" she ventured at last, fearing the worst.

"They will have been found, never fear," said her grandfather.

"It's such a pity we couldn't have a cabin," whispered her grandmother, looking around at the ragged bundles of humanity she was forced to share quarters with, for more people had boarded at Queenstown. The ship had berthed a little way off the port, and the tender had made countless trips to ferry dozens of impoverished Irish families to the ship.

"My only fear of Queenstown is that the police might have been telegraphed about our taking the boys," said Mr. Coomb. "I didn't dare breathe until we lost sight of land. I dunno if we can ever come back to Liverpool, now. We're criminals."

Debra was almost afraid of her grandparents now. The voyage was not at all what she imagined it would be. She thought they'd have a nice cabin to themselves, and that she'd be free to roam about and make friends with other girls her age, perhaps even meet a nice boy and take walks around the deck with him.

She was going further and further away from her best friend in all the world, her sister Sally. Where was she now? Perhaps she wasn't thinking of them at all as she enjoyed her freedom and her life as Mrs. Longman, her finger sporting a sparkling ring and with new clothes on her back, and going about in his carriage to see his friends.

"We had better find Papa freed when we dock," she muttered to herself as she cleaned up sick from the front of Willie's little frock for the umpteenth time. "And then we'll all come straight back again. And we'll be able to come back second-class instead of this horrible hole. Oh stop crying, Willie! You're really gettin' on my nerves."

Her grandmother was calling urgently for a basin, and she rushed away to attend her.

# CHAPTER TWENTY-ONE

Olivia and her mother went straight to the police, but there was nothing to be done. The ship had left British waters.

"Can't you telegraph the Captain?" begged Mrs. Coomb.

The constable looked at the poorly-dressed woman in front of him, her little child by her side.

"It's not possible," he said. "I'm sorry, but they've gone too far out to sea."

. . .

Maureen's last hope was gone. She and Olivia returned to their little room in Daffodil Court. It felt very empty and quiet without the noise and revelry the two little boys always made between them. There was no fire lit.

"We must go back to the hospital to see Sally," Maureen said after she had lit the fire, boiled a kettle and drunk tea. Olivia had milk and a bun. They set off again very quickly after eating.

"Now, don't you say anything at all, except to ask her how she is." Maureen instructed her. "Are you listening? Say nothing, and we'll go to Moser's on the way home for cinnamon snails."

Sally was awake this time, sitting up in bed, staring into space. She did not look like herself, Olivia thought. Her face was long. and her eyes were sad and lost. There was a vase of flowers beside her bed. She seemed pleasantly surprised to see her stepmother and Olivia.

·  ·  ·

"How did you know I was 'ere?" was her first reaction.

"There's a lot to tell you, Sally, but first—'ow are you?"

Sally looked down at the sheet and twisted it between her fingers.

"I wish I—"

"Don't say it, Sally. No matter how bad it is. God saved your life. Yes, we know why you're 'ere. And Mr. Longman is gone, isn't he?"

Sally nodded, her face becoming red, her eyes filling with tears. Olivia was astounded at the transformation in her from the person she knew before.

. . .

"I suppose you won't 'ave me back?" Sally asked Maureen in a low tone, her lip trembling.

"I will 'ave you back. We 'ave to stick together, Sally, because things have 'appened in the last two days, and we need you, and you need us."

"What sorts of things?"

Maureen began to tell her, and Sally began to weep. Olivia was again surprised. This wasn't the enraged crying she'd seen before when Sally did not get her way—this was a heartbroken, sad and helpless sobbing.

"Papa up for murder! He din't do it. He wouldn't. And our 'ouse at Crescent Court being sold—oh, it's all too much! And Grandmama, Grandpapa, and *Debra* gone to America! *Debra!*"

"And John and Willie too!" blurted Olivia, forgetting that she was supposed to say nothing. However, her mother did not chide her, only put an arm about her, drawing her close. How odd grown-up people were;

she wasn't supposed to talk at all, but when she did, her Mama knew she talked because she was hurt about her brothers going away, and so she was comforted instead of being scolded!

"John and Willie? Why?"

There was silence. Now it was Maureen's turn to weep. Sally stared at her.

"Grandmama and Grandpapa took them away from Mama." Olivia now felt she had full permission to speak.

"That was very wrong of them!" Sally exclaimed. There was a little of the old Sally in the anger.

The doctor came over.

"You're ready to be discharged, Miss Coomb. You're very lucky. You must never do that again. Next time, there might not be someone around to rescue you, putting his own life at risk."

.   .   .

"Do you know who it was, Doctor?"

"No, I do not know his name. But he came in earlier today, and said he was very glad you will be all right. You were sleeping. He left those." He nodded to the flowers. Sally turned and stared at them for a moment.

The doctor moved away, and silence fell, until Sally spoke again.

"I din't intend to fall in love with Mr. Longman, you know. It was all just for fun, at first. But I did get to love 'im. I thought he felt the same way! And that he'd marry me. I'm sorry I left 'ome the way I did, and caused you no end of worry and strife. I want to tell you something, Mother. As soon as I hit the cold water, I was sorry. I wished with all my 'eart I had not gone in. Is there a way back for me, Mother, or am I ruined?"

.   .   .

"We have to pick up what's left. And go on. We have others to think of besides ourselves." Maureen laid a hand on Olivia's head.

"I've no job. I doubt they'll take me back at the chocolate factory!"

"If you tell me what the work entails, I'll apply there. But I can't apply as a Coomb. I'll use my mother's maiden name, Enright. You can stay at 'ome for a while and teach Olivia to read and write."

They began the walk home, Sally in her dried out, wrinkled clothes and hard, still-damp boots.

"Mama, Moser's." Olivia reminded her. "You said you'd get me cinnamon snails."

"I think we'll leave it for today, Olivia. We need to get home and see to the fire and get something to eat."

. . .

"Let's get her some cinnamon snails, if she wants them," was Sally's unexpected opinion.

They turned for the bakery.


Olivia had a lot to think about that night, as she lay in bed, her little doll Mops in her arms.


Life was up and down. It was crooked and straight. It was funny and sad. Good and bad. Lucky and unlucky.


It could make you afraid.


Many things from the past two days came to her mind. Her father in prison. Sally married, Sally not married. Uncle Jimmy not rich. Jenny spending most of her life in hospital. The woman with the bloody dressing on her face. The doctor scolding Sally and telling her not to do it again. She must have left the tow-path and walked closer to the water and slipped in.

.  .  .

She heard her mother's murmuring voice, talking softly to Sally as they sat beside the fire. She caught snatches of what she was saying and they made her curious. Words like 'hunger' and 'mass graves' and 'people dropping on the way to the ship.'

"I never knowed you went through all that!" wailed Sally in a loud voice.

"Shh!" said her mother.

John and Willie couldn't hear Mama's voice. Poor John! Poor Willie!

## CHAPTER TWENTY-TWO

Olivia did not like her mother going out to work, as she was left with Sally all day. But to her surprise, Sally took more notice of her than she had ever done, and was not very bossy or cross. Sally kept house and had supper ready in the evening for when her mother came home. In the daytime, she taught Olivia her letters. She was a little stricter than Olivia would have liked, making her do her lessons and hiding Mops away during class time.

Neither of them liked to be cooped up, and they spent part of every day walking, rain or no. They went to Salisbury Dock and admired Victoria Tower with its clock on every side, they went to St. James'

Gardens, and Sally told her the story that Papa had told her, of the unfortunate Mr. Huskinsson, a Member of Parliament who on the very day that Mr. Stephenson drove his new train into Liverpool, was killed on the tracks. They looked at his monument, and Olivia thought it was a dreadful thing to happen, to go out for a day's festivities and end up dead. Life was good and bad and all in one day too.

The weather was warming, the older Coombs had been gone for several weeks. Every day when Maureen came home from work, she would ask: "Any letters?" before she even greeted Olivia.

But there were none. Upon hearing this, Maureen fell into a silent, despairing mood. She went many times a week to the police station, though she knew there was little hope.

The only joy, as usual, was when Uncle Jimmy visited. Olivia had forgiven him for not having a gold ring from the Sultan. He still told colourful stories and brought Moser's cakes and tried to jolly them along.

. . .

Mrs. Sullivan and Julia visited unexpectedly one fine evening, and the girls were delighted to see each other again, though Olivia noticed that Julia looked around her, staring at everything, the peeling walls, the rickety tables and chairs, the bed.

"Do you sleep here?" asked Julia.

"Yes."

"So what's upstairs then?" asked Julia.

"People live up there."

"Oh. Other people?"

"Yes."

"When is your Papa coming back?" was another question.

.  .  .

"When he gets out of prison."


"Why did he go to prison? Did he steal?"


"No."


"Then why?"


But Olivia would not tell her. Her mother had told her not to tell anybody what her father had been accused of, because it was all untrue, a very big mistake the American police made, but people might believe it.


"Why did your brothers go to America?"


Olivia, feeling embarrassed and a little upset, said,

.  .  .

"Because Papa wanted them there."

"Oh. Why didn't you go?"

"We're going, too," said Olivia vehemently. "We're all going, very soon. Papa wants all of us to go to America."

"If you go to America, you can't be my friend anymore."

Olivia was silent.

Olivia had made friends in Daffodil Court. Ben, Ellie and Kate had homes, but one would never think it, because they spent so much time on the streets. They were more comfortable there. They dressed in dirty rags, went barefoot summer and winter, and looked very wild, but Olivia had got used to the way they looked, and thought nothing of it now.

. . .

She took Julia out to meet them. But they didn't take to her, nor she to them. Ben pulled the ribbon from her hair, and Ellie kicked a shower of dirty pebbles over her shoes. Kate crept behind her and startled her with a big 'BOO!' and the trio laughed. Julia ran indoors and for the rest of the visit, would not budge from her mother's side. Olivia was upset, because Julia did not want to talk to her either, and they went home soon after that without Julia saying as much as goodbye. But as she went out the door, she looked back at Olivia with a fearful, disappointed expression that went to her heart.

Now Julia was gone as well as her brothers.

"Why can't somebody write?" sighed her mother, sitting at the hearth, her mind returning immediately to the matter closest to her heart. "If, God forbid, the ship had gone down, we'd 'ave heard of it. So they must have got to New York, and not bothered to write. How are my little lads? I wonder your Papa hasn't written to me. Maybe they're not allowed write letters. I have to do something, Sally. I can't stay here and do nothing. My heart is breaking.

Will you take another letter tonight? What is it, Olivia?"

"Ben pulled Julia's ribbon, and Kate and Ellie were horrid to her as well."

"Are you sure he's getting those letters, Mother?" Sally was gathering up the teacups with a clatter.

"I don't know. But if I send it to the Male Prison, New York, what can be the matter with that? How many Male Prisons can there be in New York? It's not as big as Liverpool, is it? If he's not in one, the Governor would surely have the heart to send it to another, and it having come all the way from England. Olivia, go to bed, child. It's high time you were in bed."

"Mama, Ben pulled Julia's ribbon off and ran around waving it."

. . .

"Oh, what a tormentor he is. Are you ready, Sally? Leave the washing-up."

"She wouldn't play with me, after that!"

"Don't mind about it, Olivia. They're your friends now, and Julia is spoiled anyway. Go to bed now."

Olivia took Mops and went over to the bed to put her nightgown on.

"Mama, my prayers!" she said, with reproach. Mama always heard her prayers.

"Prayers. Of course, lamb." Her mother recollected herself and came over and supervised her night prayers, tucked her in, and gave her a kiss.

"All right, Sal—are you ready? *'Dear Bertie, I hope this finds you well...'*"

# CHAPTER TWENTY-THREE

Olivia began to harbour the fear that her mother would go to America and leave her with Sally. She might not come home at all after work, and instead go to the docks and board a ship.

She was now old enough to be out on her own and so every evening she ran to Old Hall Street to meet her mother coming out of the factory, being careful when she crossed the streets and taking no shortcuts through the numerous alleys. Her mother was surprised at first, until she learned the reason.

"Promise me that you won't go to America without me," pleaded Olivia, when after three or four meetings, her mother wanted to know why she was coming to meet her.

"Dear child, I won't do that! I can't afford my own fare."

"How much is it to go to America?"

"Six guineas or thereabouts. Too dear."

"Six pounds and six shillings," said Olivia. "That's an awful lot of money, Mama."

"Are you easy now, little lamb?" her mother put an arm around her.

"Yes, Mama!"

They were silent and Olivia knew that Mama was thinking of John and Willie. And her Papa.

When they turned into the Court, Sally was looking out anxiously for them at the door. She waved. Tommy Sullivan had come with a letter from America. It had been delivered to their old house, and Tommy had been sent over with it. Sally was wild with excitement.

"It's Debra's writing! Oh quick, Mother, open it!"

Maureen tore it open with trembling fingers.

*Dear Mother, forgive my delay in writing, things have been so topsy-turvy. We arrived in New York after a desperate passage, very stormy. John and Willie are well. As for Papa, we saw him. He is still in prison awaiting Trial. He wonders he hadn't heard from you except for the letter we delivered. I am working in a rich house in New York, name of Van Dee, in Brooklyn Heights. Is there any news of Sally—Mrs. Longman as she is now. She has surely been in touch. Our address is at the top of this letter. Grandmama is well but Grandpapa is not. He has not found work. We live in a horrid place up three flights, with people below us and above us. We had a better place but had to come into this one to save money for Papa. Grandpapa engaged a lawyer to take Papa's case. It is very complicated. The man who was killed had drawn a knife on Papa and he acted in self-defence. I think the lawyer is no good.*

*I don't like it here much. I miss Liverpool and the people here are not as nice as they are at home. No time for more, love to Olivia and Uncle Jimmy.*

*Debra*

*P.S. I did not agree with John and Willie being taken from you, and I hope you recovered all right that day.*

"Oh, they are well. Thank God. But how horrid the Prison Governors must be in America! To think they never delivered any of the letters I've written!"

Maureen walked on air for the rest of the evening. Her relief knew no bounds. Sally sat and wrote a reply to Debra from herself, and one dictated by Maureen.

# CHAPTER TWENTY-FOUR

"Mrs. Coomb, you're needed urgently." The strange man dressed in a blackened overall, with smears of dirt about his face, his hat askew, had not knocked, but pushed open the door on this wet evening.

"Who are you? What's the matter?" Maureen got hurriedly to her feet.

"Begging your pardon, Ma'am. I'm Ben Watson. I works with James O'Brien. He's your brother, isn't he? He's been in a bad accident down at the docks."

There were exclamations of horror at this news, followed by flurries of activity. Mrs. Coomb got her cloak and bonnet and followed the man who said he would take her to the hospital.

Sally finished the dishes and told Olivia to go to bed, and she obeyed, but stayed awake as long as she could to hear Mama's step outside the window. It was getting dark—why was Mama out so long?

At last! She heard the light footfall pass. In another moment, the door was open. Sally was still up and the living room was bathed in a soft light.

"What's the news?"

"It's very bad, Sally. A large crate was being hoisted onto a ship, and a chain broke, and the crate fell—he was pinned underneath—taken half-dead to the hospital. He couldn't survive such an accident. He was gone an hour later." Mama began to cry softly.

Olivia jumped out of bed.

"Uncle Jimmy's dead!" she cried.

Two days later, they buried him. Everybody who knew him attended. Not only the children wept for Uncle Jimmy, but many adults.

"The world lost a ray of sunshine." Father Sheehan said in his sermon. "James' life was not an easy one, but he spread joy around as much as he could. Many a face would light up when he'd appear; and when he left, he left smiles. We're grateful for having known such a man."

Olivia helped her mother to pack Uncle Jimmy's few belongings. He had nothing of great value.

"Mama, can I have the snuff-box?" Olivia asked, holding it in her hand.

"Oh, that's really something for a boy, Olivia. But since John and Willie are so young, all right, you can have it. Mind it, though."

"I don't know what I'll keep in it," Olivia said. "Maybe my treasures." She held it to her nose to smell the tobacco because it reminded her of Uncle Jimmy. "Mama, what did you say about Uncle Jimmy before? Why was he cross with Sally being ruined?"

"Uncle Jimmy had a sweetheart, and 'er head was turned by a rich man, and the rich man left 'er. And she was ruined."

"What was the sweetheart's name?"

"Goodness, child, how curious you are! It was Lily, and she became—but it's not proper to say. But he prayed for her. I know that. I saw him in the church often, his head bowed down. I asked him once was he praying for something in particular, and he said he was praying for poor Lily. Oh, look!" She picked up something.

"What is it, Mama?"

"It's Lily's likeness. When Uncle Jimmy knew her."

Olivia examined the photo. Miss Lily was beautiful. She did not know how exactly people got ruined, but she hoped her face was not ruined.

## CHAPTER TWENTY-FIVE

Sally and Olivia were taking their daily walk one day, when Sally suggested they walk by the canal for a change.

"We 'ave to keep to the tow-path," said Olivia, skipping along.

"Of course, we'll keep to the tow-path!"

Olivia said no more. Why was Sally going to the canal? There were nicer walks. Once there, they walked for a bit, past the lock gates, then along banks with large warehouses and offices. Near one of them, Sally paused and looked towards the water. She was very quiet. There were some scattered houses along the tow-path a little farther on, and she told Olivia to sit on a bench and wait—she would be back in a while.

Olivia waited, amusing herself by making a daisy-chain. Then she got impatient and went in search of her step-sister. She was talking to a woman at a garden gate that looked out on the water. She hung back.

"It's good ter see you looking so well; I'll tell Hughie when 'e comes 'ome, that you dropped by to thank 'im. He works in that place—you see that big building there—Northern Coal. He was coming home when he saw you go in. He'll be mighty glad ter know of it, 'e wondered if you were orright."

"Thank you," Sally said. "Maybe I'll come by Sunday to thank 'im in person. I was very blessed he was to hand when I fell in."

Olivia listened with interest, then scampered back to the bench before Sally came back for her, and hung the daisy-chain around her neck.

"Now, time to get 'ome." Sally said. "I see you've been busy."

The following Sunday, Olivia heard Sally tell her mother that she had plans to look up an old friend, and that she wouldn't accompany them on their walk. Olivia did not mind, she loved to have her mother to herself. But was Hughie an old friend, then, or was Sally telling a fib?

# CHAPTER TWENTY-SIX

M rs. Henley stayed up until Hughie came home. He had walked Miss Coomb back to Daffodil Court. She was a little worried.

He came in and was surprised to find she had not gone to bed.

"What is it, Ma?"

"It's her, Hughie. Miss Coomb. She's a nice girl an' all, but is she in 'er right mind? She jumped into the canal. You took 'er out, and now you've gone all dotty about 'er."

"Oh, Ma. She din't jump in. She was out for a walk, and her hat blew off, and when she reached to get it, she jumped forward to try to reach it—that's what she told me."

"Hmmm. You were sure she jumped in that night. Some fellow broke 'er heart, that's what I think."

"Oh no, Ma. Nothing like that. It's as I told you."

"Well I do 'ope so, Hugh. The Bank is a funny place to go fer a walk at night, though."

"I do like 'er, Ma. She's comely."

"If you say so, Hugh. Well I'm off to bed. Blow out the candle."

'Yes, Ma."

Hugh was thirty years old. He had good regular work at the coal house and had some money saved to settle down, but until he met Sally, he hadn't wanted to settle with anybody. Jumping in to rescue her had given him a powerful feeling for her. And when he visited the hospital, and saw her lying there, her face snow-white, her eyes closed in sleep, her fair hair spread over the pillow, he had known that he was in love. But apart from her name, he didn't know anything else. But it seemed that Miss Coomb felt the same about him as he did about her!

When she'd found him out, he was very pleased indeed.

He thought she had jumped into the water, but today she had told him what had really happened. Come to think of it, it was nearly dark so it was easy for him to make that mistake. She jumped for her hat, and fell in.

# CHAPTER TWENTY-SEVEN

Olivia enjoyed going to meet her mother after work and walking home with her, so even after her fears about her vanishing had gone, she kept it up, waiting for her mother outside the gate, by the railing.

Her mother appeared in the bobbing of bonnets exiting the factory door moments after the horn sounded, and she fell into step beside her.

"You wouldn't believe what happened today, Olivia. Mr. Slater brought his son in to see the factory. He's about ten or eleven, I'd say, a nice, gentle lad, I thought. And I was right! For just when he was passing, I dropped some beans that I was just about to put into the roasting oven, and he stopped by and helped me pick them up, and very polite he was too."

But after a moment she said,

"It's too bad he'll end up like the rest of them."

"What do you mean, Mama?"

"Greedy. That's what I mean. They're all greedy, these factory owners."

"All of them, Mama?"

"Maybe there are some that aren't. But the Slaters are. They put a paste into the chocolate mix, it isn't chocolate, but people think it's chocolate."

"Oh, Mama!"

"Don't tell anybody what I said, or I'll lose my position."

"Oh no, Mama. I won't."

"I have a few pennies," her mother said then. "Let's go by Moser's and buy some pastries." She dropped the pennies into Olivia's hand.

But as they rounded the corner, they saw an old woman sitting on a doorstep, her face dirty, her hand out to them. Her mother's steps slowed and stopped. Olivia's fist tightened over her pennies.

"Olivia." Mrs. Coomb did not have to tell her what to do. She opened her palm and gave her pennies to the old woman, who thanked her over and over as she got up and went to Moser's to buy herself some day-old bread.

"Don't ever pass a hungry person, Olivia," said her mother as they went along without their pastries. "That's Jesus, in disguise."

# CHAPTER TWENTY-EIGHT

"Our boy is a softie," said Mr. Edward Slater, speaking to his wife in his study, where they had been checking accounts. "Today, a female hand dropped some beans and he stopped to help her retrieve them. He's spent too much time with my mother. Women coddle him. I'm sending him to public school. Eton is to be the place."

"What are you saying, Edward? You know I haven't coddled him, that can be laid at your mother's door. And how can you talk like this of your child? I don't like to think of Franklin fetching and carrying for senior boys," said his wife crossly. *"Fagging,* they call it. I object to Eton."

"No, Franklin is to go to Eton. I am only sorry I can't say that I went there myself, but my parents didn't have the kind of awareness of the world that I have. My father was happy to make sweets all day and leave all the business to *your* father. How I wish he'd had a bit more thought to the future, for my education was very deficient, and I doubt I will ever be chosen to stand for election now."

"But Edward—there are day schools here in Liverpool, why not think of those? And they would be much cheaper! Why lay out a large amount of money for an education he can get cheaper?"

"No, Eton it will be, if I can get him in. We don't hob-nob with anybody of note. Our son needs connections to be a great man in the world. The Earls of Sefton send their boys to Eton, The Baronet Hogg's sons—he of India!—attend Eton. The son and heir to the Dukedom of Argyle is on the roll! Every other name in Eton is double-barrelled. With our son attending, we shall get to meet very important people on King George's Birthday on the fourth of June, which they celebrate out of doors on the river, with cricket and picnics. Think of it, Jemima. Can you picture yourself parading about dressed in a—a very expensive gown, with a parasol, and being introduced to the wives of those who run the British Empire, and the mothers who rocked the cradle of England's future great men?"

"What an imagination you have, Edward! I don't hanker after finery, it's expensive to keep up with the fashions, and women's chatter bores me. I find that women know nothing of business, and those women you mention aren't likely to appreciate how my thoughts run on cocoa prices in Ethiopia!"

"But you can put up with it, for Franklin's sake."

"I suppose I can. But he had better marry well. He can marry anybody he chooses as long as she has money. I don't care much for title, but money—yes. She must bring a pot of gold."

"I wonder how Henry will get on," said Mr. Slater, his mind distracted for a moment by the nephew he wanted to forget. "When we stipulated that he not set up in Liverpool, we didn't mean that he had to go to India!" he laughed at his own joke. "Do they eat chocolate there? I imagine it would melt."

"I told you, Edward, he's in Customs. It will suit him better than making confits and bonbons."

A little pause ensued.

"So, we are agreed on Eton?"

She was convinced. The bell was pulled, and Franklin was summoned to learn his fate.

# CHAPTER TWENTY-NINE

W inter was in. Daffodill Court was washed with rain from overflowing gutters and lakes of mud bathing the street. And a letter from Debra in mid-December brought the very worst news that it was possible for them to receive.

*Dear Mother and Sally,*

*Papa was found guilty. The judge did not think he acted in self-defence and he sentenced him to execution. So my father's life was taken on October 12th. We are devastated. We were allowed to see him the day before and he had wrote you a letter that I enclose. He kissed the boys goodbye and said he would see them in Heaven. They were crying and John understood what he meant.*

Maureen grasped the enclosure and read it while Sally continued with the letter. It was an affectionate note from Bertie, telling her to be strong for the children, and asserting his innocence. He finished by giving her his love forever and ever and he'd see her in Heaven. She sat by the fire, crying bitterly. Olivia climbed on her lap and cried too.

Sally thrust Debra's letter toward her. "You had better read this, Mother!"

*Grandpapa had a stroke, and he's not expected to live. Grandmama in very poor health. I have no work as I have to look after everybody. I cannot look after the boys anymore. There is an organisation here who can send them to the country to be adopted. I hope you are in agreement with this plan, unless you can send the fare for them to be sent back. Every penny we have is gone on the lawyers and now on doctors.*

"What is she thinking of," shrieked Maureen, jumping up and hastily setting Olivia on her feet, "sending the boys to be adopted to God knows where! I must go—I must raise the money to go to America and bring my boys home!"

"And take me!" exclaimed Olivia, clutching her skirts. But to her shock and heartbreak, her mother shook her head.

"I can't take you, lamb. You stay here, and go and live with Sally when she marries Mr. Henley."

Olivia collapsed in loud crying. This was a promise broken!

"I can't afford to take you," Mama pleaded with her to understand. "For I have to return with the boys. As it is, I'll have to borrow money somehow. And I will be staying in the most 'orrible places you can imagine, we've heard enough about New York now to know that it's full of dirt and rubbish and cockroaches. No, you will stay 'ere with Sally, where you'll be safe, and I'll return with John and William straight away—we'll not delay a day in New York— after paying our respects at Papa's grave—we'll be upon our way."

"What about Debra?" asked Sally, with belligerence, her tears flowing fast for her Papa. "It seems to me you care little for my father's fate, *and* you're only concerned with your own children, not Debra! Who does she have now, with Grandfather and Grandmother ill? They might die soon! She's only sixteen years old! You must bring her back as well! And how can I marry at Christmas when I'm in mourning? You never cared for Papa! Never!"

There followed a bitter, vicious quarrel. The letter bore such evil news that the three persons, but Maureen and Sally in particular, had been thrown into a great grief, fright and panic, completely unable to console each other, and only able to find relief in blame and insults.

"Oh God," pleaded Olivia, in tears, watching her mother and Sally almost come to blows. Her mother had taught her many prayers for many needs. "Dear Jesus, come and bring Your peace."

A little pause ensued—a small quiet—when the two women seemed at last to glimpse the other's pain, and they fell on each other in sorrow, apologising, crying, and saying they had not meant a word of what had been said, that the shock of the letter had hit all of them like a thunderbolt.

Thankfully, their upstairs neighbour, hearing the commotion and knowing that there was bad news, came down the outside staircase with a pot of tea. She was a widow named Mrs. Polk who lived there with her two sons, and knew all of the family's sorrows, as they knew hers. She got out the cups and sat the family down and made them drink it hot and sweet.

## CHAPTER THIRTY

"I'm going to confide in Mr. Slater, and ask him for a loan," Maureen said flatly an hour later. She considered this for a time. "He knows me as Enright, though. If he gives me a note for the bank, it will be invalid. Oh, what am I to do? Nothing to sell, or pawn. Jimmy is gone. My cousin Peg is nearly as poor as I am. Can the Henleys help, Sally? No? I thought not."

"Mama, do you want to pawn Uncle Jimmy's snuff box?" Olivia asked.

"No, child. It wouldn't fetch enough."

Olivia was relieved. She kept pretty pebbles in it and a seashell that Julia had brought her from Blackpool once.

Olivia was still distraught that she was not to go, but at the same time, she still thought her mother would relent and bring her. She remembered now something her mother told her.

"Mama, you remember the boy?"

"What boy?"

"Mr. Slater's son who helped you pick up the beans."

Mama smiled. "Bless you, little lamb, but he won't have any money! You can't go ask children for money, anyway."

But Olivia could not put it out of her head. It was near to Christmas, and people were good at Christmas. She said so to her mother, and refused to leave the subject alone, until her mother began to think around it.

"There's old Mrs. Slater," she said thoughtfully. "She's a good, kind woman, or so I've heard. I could go to her. Yes, that's the way to go. I'm not ashamed to beg. Come on, Olivia, I'll take you to Slaters with me."

Olivia felt ripples of hope in her heart. Perhaps Mrs. Slater would give money for her to go as well!

"There's no time to be lost, so we'll go now."

It was past eight o'clock and they donned cloaks and bonnets and set out at a great pace for Randal Hall, where she knew the old couple, the Slaters, lived.

The butler of Randal Hall looked upon the mother and child with great annoyance, it was late, he protested, too late! He was just about to lock up the house!

"I work for the Slater's son, Mr. Edward, and I'm in the greatest need," pleaded Maureen.

They were shown upstairs to a warm drawing room where an elderly couple sat, together with the boy named Franklin, who was occupied at the table in cutting stamps from envelopes. Olivia looked at his activity with curiosity.

But Mr. Slater had white bushy eyebrows which went up and down, so Olivia could not stop looking at them. Mrs. Slater had a pink shawl with flowers on it, and a white frilly cap with pink bows.

All listened carefully to what Mrs. Coomb—for she had given her real name—had to say. She worked in the Roasting room of the factory and had come to them in the greatest hope. They appeared shocked, distressed and sympathetic as she told her story, without embellishment or unnecessary emotion. The words spoke for themselves.

"Perhaps you may think we are not deserving, as my husband has been executed, but it was for something he didn't do. As a mother, Mrs. Slater, I beg you to put yourself in my place. My children kidnapped from me—indeed you can ask the police at Rose Hill and Seel Street—they 'ave tried to help me, to no avail. Now my boys are in danger of disappearing into the great vast continent of America, to *strangers* —they'll be as dead to me—I will never see them again!" Her voice quavered as she broke down.

By now the tears were rolling down Olivia's cheeks and mother and daughter clung together.

Mr. and Mrs. Slater exchanged a long look, with Franklin looking on with interest, his scissors laid aside for now.

The couple had been married so long that no words were needed between them. They were in complete agreement. Mr. Slater cleared his throat.

"There will be a packet leaving for America the day after tomorrow—the Inman Line—a very quick passage, I can assure you, as the ship is Iron Screw— I will send my man first thing in the morning to Water Street, to book your passage to New York, for *you* must, at the soonest, go to the police station and to your church. The first, to obtain a letter to say that the boys were taken from you by force, and the second, for their baptismal certificates, to show that you are indeed their mother, and I would advise you also, to obtain from your priest, a letter verifying *your* identity—your marriage certificate."

"Have you any travel clothes, Mrs. Coomb? I shall supply you with some, if not. I have some black worsted—for I see you are in mourning—suitable to be made up into a travel habit. We shall get to making them right away, you are about the size of my housemaid."

Maureen could have fallen on her knees in gratitude and kissed the feet of the old couple. She hugged the packet of cash to her chest, thanked them over and over. She thought that Mr. Slater was next to God in knowledge and wisdom, and Mrs. Slater in kindness and practicality.

"Can I go too?" Olivia asked Mrs. Slater in a small voice. The old lady looked at Mrs. Coomb for guidance on how to answer.

"It's not possible," murmured Maureen. "I shall get on faster on my own."

Mrs. Slater nodded with sagacity.

"Speed is of the utmost importance. Mama will come back soon, dear."

Olivia began to cry, whereupon Mrs. Slater said:

"Have you got a pretty stamp, Franklin, that you could let her have?"

He got up from the table. "I say, take these two—yellow and sort of purple."

Olivia took the stamps, stared at them in a mixture of puzzlement and admiration, then clutched her little hand around them.

"Does Master Franklin collect stamps?" exclaimed Maureen. "I'll bring you back stamps from America!"

"If you could get one with Benjamin Franklin on it, I'd be very well pleased!" he said with eagerness.

"Ooh," said Maureen, who had never heard of the gentleman. "I will keep my eye out for one of Mr. Franklin, then!"

Olivia was very silent on the way home. Her mother was going to America alone after all. She was being left behind. It did not bode well for her. She was very, very unhappy.

Her mother did not notice—all of her thoughts were of the morrow—the early rising to get to the police and to the church; and collecting the bare essentials she would take with her. She must write to Debra directly to tell her to keep the boys with her—though she would arrive in America almost as soon as the letter!

Olivia held the stamps in her hand and then licked them and stuck them on her bedpost.

# CHAPTER THIRTY-ONE

nd so, it was all done very quickly—they saw Mama off from the landing stage that led to the ship, the *Manchester*. There was one last, long and sad embrace, and then she joined the flock of other passengers surging toward the door. Sally gripped Olivia's hand. Mama looked back at them and waved once before she turned. The ship swallowed her. Olivia's tears were very copious. The girls went to the quayside scanning everybody on the deck of the *Manchester*. At last! There she was! Mama waved and waved and waved. The horn blasted, the ship began to glide away, Mama became a speck and disappeared. Olivia watched the ship vanish out of sight and then Sally brought her to Moser's and bought her cinnamon snails and a bun.

She returned home to cry and cry, until Sally's patience was tried.

"Your Ma's not dead, Livvie. She's coming back. My ma will never come back. Now dry those tears; we have to go get mournin' clothes made. We 'ave to mourn our Papa. I'm an orphan now, do you know?"

Christmas brought no joy without Mama. Sally was to have got married, but the wedding was postponed until May. And there was another move, for there was no money to pay rent. The Henleys had a small spare room, and here it was that Sally and Olivia went just a week later, to the little cottage on Canal Bank, near the coal warehouse where Hughie worked.

Sally found work as a domestic servant in a nearby home. She hated it, though she had Sundays off. While she was at work Olivia was left alone all day with old Mrs. Henley, and there were few children about, so she had no friends. Her heart was heavy.

On the Sunday after Christmas, they had unexpected visitors. Mr. and Mrs. Slater, evidently very curious for news, had found them. They were accompanied by Franklin, who strolled out by the canal with his grandfather while Sally and Mrs. Henley, who was overwhelmed by the company, drank tea with the lady visitor.

Olivia had been out at the towpath, watching the coal barges go by, still feeling forlorn and sad. She waved to the bargemen, who waved back. She turned to see Master Slater and his grandfather approach. They nodded a greeting.

"Do you like to come out here to watch the barges?" the old man asked, his white eyebrows shooting up.

"This is the first time I've done it," she said, a little shyly.

"I would be very careful if I were you, these paths are very slippery. Little girls like you could fall in," said the old man, his white eyebrows coming down and going up again.

"Oh, my sister fell in once."

"Oh, dear. Was she all right?"

"Yes, she was pulled out, and she is all right now. She ran away to get married and fell into the canal."

A muffled snort came from Master Franklin, whose boyish mind conjured a bride, in all her finery, tumbling into the water and having to be fished out dripping wet.

"What misfortune! Was her intended husband with her at the time?" asked old Mr. Slater quizzically, one eyebrow up now.

"I don't think so, because if he was, then Mr. Henley wouldn't have had to jump in to pull her out."

"And—did she get married after?"

"No, because Mr. Longman went back to—I don't know—the North."

"Mr. Longman, was that his name?" Two eyebrows went up again.

"Yes, Mr. Longman."

"Was Mr. Longman a bargeman?"

"Oh no. He was a gentleman. He had a horse and gave her lots of gifts, he gave her a beautiful purple hat, and a pearl bracelet, only I broke that, by accident."

Nothing more was said, except,

"And was that your sister Sally we met in the house, who is going to marry Mr. Henley?"

"Yes! I like him more than I like Mr. Longman. I met him once only, and he didn't say anything."

# CHAPTER THIRTY-TWO

It was an astounding story. The old couple made the connection on the way home— Henry Longman's sudden disappearance had a cause they never had guessed. This unfortunate girl Sally who perhaps had tried to drown herself after she was jilted. They sat forward, with Mr. Slater driving, and Franklin sat to the rear. They forgot he was there, and he heard every word.

"I feel more responsible for the family now that I know there's a connection," said Mrs. Slater. "What a horrible tale! Henry never had any intention of marrying Sally Coomb."

"We should take an interest and do what we can to aid this poor family."

The old couple had been active all of their lives, and found retirement tedious. Edward did not want his father involved in the business and he rarely went there. Mrs. Slater liked to help people, had numerous charities and was Chairwoman of the Society for Aid to Stranded Foreign Sailors.

"Sally is going to be married, so that's her settled. But what of the child Olivia? Suppose it happens that her mother never comes back? Misfortune can occur—illnesses, accidents—America is very far away. I would like to hear the full history of Henry Longman and Sally," she went on. "But I cannot ask without offending delicacy. And if she is to marry and put the sorry episode behind her, then there's no finding out. I do hope Henry did not take advantage. I will assume the best, that he did not. That he behaved like a gentleman, but when it came to it, took fright when Sally got it into her head that they were to marry. Has Edward mentioned anything of this affair to you? Did he even know of it?"

"If he knew, he mentioned not a thing. But he's silent in general, as you know."

"He's still adding that *taft* to the confection," Mrs. Slater said with distaste. "We left him too much with the Collys when he was at an impressionable age."

"Oh dear," Mrs. Slater said a few moments later. "I forgot that Franklin is behind us. Are we to drop you off at your parents', Frank?" she asked in a louder voice.

"Yes, Grandmama, if you please."

"And you are to return to school tomorrow. We have something for you before you go."

"Oh, thanks!" he grinned, his mind full of the tuck shop.

The discussion between his grandparents had been interesting. He had no knowledge of love matters, but it seemed that his cousin, whom he'd never liked, led this girl up the garden path and she tried to kill herself—he found it amazing that a girl would throw herself into the canal over Henry! Women were very strange creatures.

# CHAPTER THIRTY-THREE

The weeks went by slowly, very slowly. At last a letter with a foreign stamp was delivered to Canal Bank. Olivia jumped up and practically climbed upon Sally to glimpse it.

"What's in it? What does she say?" she asked, in an agony of impatience, her whole body quivering with anxiety. "Is she coming home soon? Oh, *when* is Mama coming home?"

Sally made only a half-hearted attempt to shake her off.

"Let me see ... she is with Debra, but John and Willie —" Sally swallowed. "They were put on a train to Penn—Penn-sylvania to find homes, and Mother is following them there ... she will write—she sends love and kisses to you. She's not coming home, not yet."

"She's not—she's not coming home." Olivia replayed the words in her mind over and over. The word 'yet' meant nothing.

Mama was not coming home.

She jumped away from Sally and ran outside. Away, away from the house, past the warehouses, past other houses, to strange places off from the towpath, to where there were even fewer houses, and more fields, and into a woods, deeper into the trees, until she fell down from exhaustion. She sobbed until sleep overcame her.

When she woke, it was getting dark. The trees loomed above her, birds twittered and swooped in and out of the branches. Two thoughts were in her head immediately.

Her mother was not coming home. The thought scalded her heart.

The second thought was that she did not know her way back. This made her fearful. She was cold and hungry. She began to walk along a rough pathway, but every corner brought new shadows, more trees and more terrors. She ran, stumbled, fell, got herself up and ran again. Brambles and thorns scratched at her bare feet and legs, she was hardly conscious of any pain. She ran and ran, stumbling, falling, getting herself up again, and running again, not knowing where she was going.

After a time, the birds settled in their nests, their young fed. Darkness had fallen, and she was alone. She stopped for a moment to look about and saw a set of twinkling lights between the trees, how far or how near, she could not tell. She made a beeline for them, scraping her legs and even her arms to make her way through thickets, and came out of the woods to see the dim outline of a house. She heard animal sounds. The moon came up and she saw she was in a meadow with a flock of sheep and their lambs. Near her lay a ewe with her lamb by her side. She remembered how her Mama used to call her 'lamb.' She lay down beside the sheep, who did not seem to notice her. Edging closer to the warm woolly back, finding the animal smell strangely comforting, she fell asleep again.

The farm dogs awoke her at dawn, barking madly in her face. She cried out in panic. The ewe and her lamb had left. Above the excited faces of the sheepdogs, she beheld a very old wrinkled face with a hat.

# CHAPTER THIRTY-FOUR

"The girl is mute. Is she deaf also?" asked Mr. Parsons, one of the Board of Guardians in Brownlow Hill Workhouse.

"No, she understands what is said." Dr. Lambert answered. "She didn't respond when asked her name, so we supplied a pencil and paper, and she wrote: *OLIV COB.* I would think she probably meant, *Olive Cobb.* She's young to have learned how to spell properly, and her clothes indicate that, while not an urchin, her rank is decidedly low."

"So, she is not an imbecile." Mr. Parson wrote in his book. "It's not easy to classify a child who cannot speak but can hear. One doesn't know if there is a deficiency of understanding. What else?"

"She's covered in scratches and bruises. Nurse Shaw has bathed them and applied bandages to the worst, and she has a bad cold."

"Her age?"

"She wrote the number 6."

"Her parents?"

"She wrote nothing, but looked very unhappy indeed, then drew a ship. Her drawings are superior for a child."

"A ship, eh? Curious. Or maybe not. Every child in Liverpool draws ships. Address?"

"Not a clue, I'm afraid."

"Nothing with her to identify her."

"No, as the porter said, a farmer carried her to the gate in his arms. He found her among the sheep in the meadow. She most likely came through the woods."

"After she's discharged from the Infirmary, she can go to the Girls Section. Why, Doctor, would a child hear, but not say a word?"

"Either her larynx has a loss of function or it's something in her mind, an experience so frightening to her that she lost the power of speech."

"Very strange."

"If it is the latter, it may return."

"Let us hope so. A child with such a handicap cannot hope to go anywhere in life. She may be with us forever."

# CHAPTER THIRTY-FIVE

"I still don't know what to write to Mother," Sally said, as she sewed her wedding dress with her future mother-in-law. "How can I tell her that Livvy's run away? She'll say I ill-treated 'er. But I 'ave to tell her *sometime*. But I think the worst 'as happened. She doted on her, spoiled her, she did, not that I want to say anything bad about poor little Livvy, if she's dead, but she shouldn't have run off like she did that day."

"Thank God Mrs. Coomb got one of her sons back safe and sound," said Mrs Henley. "That must 'ave been a very joyous reunion, at least she will 'ave him, to console her in her sorrow, when she does get the news about poor little Livvy."

"So she's settling over there, in this place called Scranton, waiting to get Willie, cos his new parents won't give 'im up." said Sally, a little crossly. "What is it about America anyway? What's so special about America? Debra isn't coming home neither. That makes me angry. I'd always set my 'eart on Debra being my bridesmaid."

"There seems to be a great deal of work to be 'ad in America, all the same. After your grandparents passed away—so sad that was—she picked up a situation no bother, and it sounds like a good 'ouse." Mrs. Henley said, "And what about her young man, the fellow Hans from Germany? He sounds like a very decent chap with a good trade, and never out of work."

Sally made no reply.

"Do you want the little bows like so, Sally, or a little further apart?" asked Mrs. Henley then.

"They're fine the way you're doing them."

Sally put down her work and took up the letter again that had come that day from America. It was more of a packet than a letter, and the postman had been very careful to put it into Sally's hands.

*"There's money in it,"* he had said almost in a whisper. *"We can always tell if there's money in a packet. Thank Heaven it got this far without interference! I wanted to be sure you got it."* He hung about, no doubt hoping she'd open it in his presence, but she'd thanked him and shut the door.

"Olivia's fare to America." Sally said again. "And instructions to find a good family for 'er to travel with. She thought of everything. If only Olivia would turn up suddenly, at the door, I'd be easy. I'd buy her passage, pick out a nice family who was travelling, and put 'er on the next ship with 'em. But I'm not optimistic. I could've followed 'er that day, but I thought she was only gone a little way and would come back. The Constable was no 'elp. I bet if she was a rich child, he'd 'ave made an effort. Just telling me, like that, that children go missing every day and try the 'ospitals and Brownlow Hill. Nobody 'ad an Olivia Coomb."

"It's likely she slipped into the water," said Mrs. Henley. "Poor little mite."

"I'll wait another while afore I write to Mother," Sally said. "A few weeks maybe, then we'll be sure."

# CHAPTER THIRTY-SIX

"**I** wonder how Mrs. Coomb is getting on, and whether she found her children." said Mrs. Slater, her needle dipping in and out of a shirt she was making for the Stranded Foreign Sailors. "I thought she might write to us."

"

If somebody has to write for her, she may only communicate with her stepdaughter Sally," said her husband.

"Well then, we should go to Miss Sally to find out how she is faring."

. . .

"You'll have to excuse me on this trip. The gout."

"Of course, dear, and black cherries are said to be good, if Cullen could scour the markets for some."

The following day, Mrs. Slater set out alone for the Canal Bank. Sally was at work, but Mrs. Henley gave her the entire sorry tale.

"Missing! How can that be? The child ran away? And —you think she slipped into the water? Oh dear, what a catastrophe! Her mother's heart will be broken!"

When Mrs. Slater heard that Miss Coomb had not *yet* written to her stepmother, and was waiting on the slim chance that the child turned up, she was immediately anxious.

"Oh dear, no. That will not do. A mother has to know these things without delay. But she is settling over there, you say? Strange! What does everybody see in America? We did give her the fare to get herself and her boys home, but if it's better spent on settling herself down in—where did you say —*Scanting?* I have no objection. Mr. Slater will be very happy also that she has been successful in her quest to have at least one son with her again. But Olivia lost! I will make enquiries. And if you could be so good as to provide me with an address for Mrs. Coomb in Scanting, Pennsylvania, I would be very grateful."

Mrs. Henley rummaged in a drawer and produced the address.

Mrs. Slater returned home and wrote a letter that evening. No matter if Sally Coomb could not bring herself to do it; she would take on the unpleasant task of informing Mrs. Coomb that her daughter Olivia was missing. As she had provided the funds for the voyage, she felt that she had some responsibility.

. . .

She would also have to say, but in a very delicate way, that the general opinion was that Olivia may have slipped into the canal. It would be the worst news any mother could get, and Maureen would go out of her mind with distress.

# CHAPTER THIRTY-SEVEN

I t was July before a letter arrived from Scranton, Pennsylvania.

*Dear Mrs. Slater,*

*Permit me to introduce myself. My name is Mrs. Marsden, and my husband (an attorney) and I are assisting poor Mrs. Coomb with her various concerns. After the news of yesterday, which came in your letter, she collapsed and is now in bed under a doctor's care. She has urged me to write in her stead, as she feels incapable of even dictating a letter.*

. . .

*She does not believe her daughter is dead (a very natural reaction in that no remains have been found) and urges a thorough search for her. She says that her stepdaughter Sally does not have the connections to move Police to mount an exhaustive search, so she begs your intervention.*

*Mrs. Coomb has to go to Law to force the new 'parents' of Willie—a charming little cherub, you will agree, to give him up to her. As soon as she is successful, she will return. She asks me to thank you for your generous gift.*

The letter went on to give some details about how Mrs. Coomb had been offered work in a cookhouse and how her accommodation was arranged.

Mrs. Slater put down the letter. Mrs. Coomb over-estimated her influence. She did not know any powerful people. But she had a few ideas. She could place advertisements in the newspapers and could make personal enquiries at Brownlow Hill. She would do a thorough search. But she was not optimistic about a child who went missing near a canal. Her husband had shaken his head and recalled that he had seen the danger last Christmas.

. . .

Poor Mrs. Coomb might have to accept the unthinkable.

CHAPTER THIRTY-EIGHT

# 1 858

One year later, Olivia was used to being called Olive Cobb and it did not upset her. She felt she was another girl anyway. Olivia Coomb was dead— maybe—and Olive Cobb was in her place. Olive Cobb could not speak. Olive Cobb had no mother or father or sisters or brothers or home or toys. Olive Cobb was very sad. Olive had few friends and had learned to amuse herself. She listened a great deal to what other people said around her. She went to school and heard the teacher, but she could not ask questions. She never read passages from books to the class. She was often forgotten, but there were nice girls like Polly and Sue who chattered to her; even though she smiled, she could not answer them at all. She drew pictures to ask for what she wanted. She drew all the time. The schoolmistress had arranged for her to carry a slate and chalk with her always.

She drew Olivia Coomb's life—the girl who was surely dead—or taken by the fairies—so that everybody knew it by now. Her house in Crescent Court. Her father coming home with his kit on his shoulder. Her two baby brothers. Sally—cross Sally! Debra, a little less cross. And of course, Olivia's mother—a gentle sad face. She drew Uncle Jimmy, large as life and smiling. She drew the Sultan giving him a gold ring, though she knew it was just a story. She did not know how a Sultan dressed but she thought he would wear a crown and long robes. The girls crowded around and wanted to know more, so she drew Uncle Jimmy in some of the other Tall Tales she had heard. She drew Julia with a big pearl bracelet on her head. She drew hats with feathers and she drew Mr. Longman on a horse. She knew who these people were but nobody else did. She drew hospital beds and nurses with their funny veils and Jenny.

For the first year, those were her drawings. Then, she began to draw whatever was around her—she drew horrid pictures of Mrs. Bridge, who was horrid to the girls, and made her companions laugh before she quickly rubbed them out with her sleeve.

She wished she could speak, but the words were locked up. They were under a frozen river, were her words. They were there but she could not go under the ice for them.

There were prayers, and the Master tried to get her to say them, but he gave up. But there were some very nice prayers and she was glad to hear the others say them. Like the one about the Lord being her shepherd. And crossing the valley of darkness—she remembered the night she ran through the dark woods and how ill she had been for a week afterward, her legs bandaged. She pondered these words in her perpetual silence. There were other beautiful stories and words too. Scenes from the Bible that she thought about a great deal. She pictured Daniel in the lion's den being protected by God. She could not talk to her friends, or anybody, but she could talk as much as she liked to God, and she did, because God heard her words without her having to say them, God could get under the ice.

*God* was her best friend.

# CHAPTER THIRTY-NINE

E dward Slater was annoyed. His mother was paying him and Jemima a visit, and though he at least was very fond of her, she did not understand anything about business, and her request was very unreasonable.

"Mother, this Sally Coomb—now Henley—you talk of—yes I remember her. She came to us at night to ask for our Henry, and the following day, I dismissed her sister. Now, you are telling me that the woman we knew as Maureen Enright was *their* stepmother? And you want me to take her back, after she disappeared?"

"The circumstances, Edward, the circumstances! Where is your heart? You have to temper business with mercy and charity. Your father always did. You had no right to dismiss her sister, putting the family in a very bad way. What could the stepmother do, except to apply for her job, and give a false name?"

Edward ignored the question, but Jemima said,

"Henry was a dull fellow."

"He may have been dull, but he led Sally Coomb on. He led her to expect marriage, and then he disappeared. She could have been ruined, and what did he, or you, care? The girl tried to drown herself."

Edward rose and paced the carpet in front of the fireside screen.

"A gentleman does not take advantage of a girl of lower rank if he has no intention of marriage. It's selfish and reprehensible," lectured his mother.

"The girl, I suppose, has to bear no blame." Jemima said icily.

"A poor girl's head can be easily turned. You should be ashamed of Henry Longman. I am asking as a special favour. This is close to my heart. Take Mrs. Coomb back when she returns, which will be soon, for she has secured the return of her second son from his adoptive parents at last."

"Really, Mother. You get too involved with your cases."

"This is the first time I have asked you to employ someone."

"If she's coming back, she will want then to look for her daughter, and how will she have the time to work? She will miss days, and want to go home early, and so on."

"*I* am looking for Olivia." Though a full year had passed, Mrs. Slater was still placing advertisements and posting bills.

Edward raised his eyes to the ceiling while Jemima gave a sigh of impatience.

"I did not want to bring this up," Mrs. Slater said then. "But because you have no time for your own son, his grandfather and I have supplied him with all the attention due to him from his parents. He does not even get letters from you when he's away at Eton! We write every week. I do not resent the care of him in the holidays; he's great company and cheers our lives. Perhaps he may wonder why you don't have time for him, and that as soon as he arrives home from Eton, he's packed off to our house within forty-eight hours. Well?"

"What you are saying, Mother, is that you are owed." Jemima said.

She was silent.

"I suppose we can take Mrs. Coomb back." Edward conceded.

"Thank you."

She pulled the bell and the servant showed her out. Going home in the carriage, she was chagrined. How had her son turned out so differently from his good, kind father?

But she had no time to dwell. Maureen Coomb was due to return soon, and she wanted to find little Olivia before she arrived.

# CHAPTER FORTY

Olivia was coming out of the schoolroom one day, her slate in her hand, when she heard someone call her name. Her real name. *Olivia,* not Olive.

She wheeled around in amazement to see Julia Sullivan running toward her, and Julia was in a workhouse uniform.

"Oh Olivia, I'm so glad to see you! I don't know anybody at all!"

Instantly, Olivia felt *Olive Cobb* drain away. *Olive Cobb* faded, and Olivia Coomb hastened back.

"Julia," she said, forcing the word from her mouth. The ice began to melt and the words began to bubble up. "What are you doing here?"

"She can talk!" the ripple went around the group of girls who were in the vicinity. "Olive Cobb can talk!"

"Who's Olive Cobb?" asked Julia, puzzled.

"They called me that. I don't know why."

"Why are they saying you couldn't talk?"

"Because I couldn't."

Olivia took her arm. "Julia, why are you in here?"

"You didn't hear about us?"

"No, not a word."

"My Papa died."

"So did mine. In America."

"Our house burned down. Papa forgot the—the—I don't know, but the man said we couldn't get any money. Mama and I came here today. She went into the Women's Section. Deirdre is married in Great Howard Street. She and George have only a room. She's going to take Mama and me soon, after they move. Until then, I have to be here. Is it horrid here? I hate it! But why are you here?"

By now they were surrounded by a great circle, all gathered to hear the dumb girl speak.

Olivia explained the entire story and at the end of it, the pauper attendants had gathered, summoned Mrs. Bridges, who instead of being happy for her, accused her

.

"I knew you could talk! You could talk all along, you little brat! You were malingering for attention, weren't you? Give me that slate this instant!" She took it and smashed it on the ground.

"I'm afraid of her," Julia whispered, her face ashen.

Matron came next, and Olivia was summoned to her office, where *Olive Cobb* loomed again for a moment, just a moment, so frightened was she, but now that the ice had melted, *Olive Cobb* couldn't come back, and Olivia Coomb stood in Matron's office while she sat and looked through a file.

Matron asked her several questions, gently enough, probing where she had come from. Olivia could not remember the address of the cottage on Canal Bank, so she had to stay in the workhouse until Sally Coomb could be found. But she didn't want to go back to Canal Bank, to the old woman. Here in the workhouse, she had Julia, and they were again the best of friends.

"I'm sorry Ben Mahon pulled your ribbons that day. He's a brat," she said to her after they were reunited at suppertime.

"Oh, that doesn't matter. Do you still have Mops?"

# CHAPTER FORTY-ONE

The doctor was jubilant at the news that the little dumb girl had found her voice again. He had a distant cousin who was a journalist in the Mercury, and before long, a story was run upon the extraordinary tale.

Mr. Slater saw it as he perused the newspaper in his study.

*An extraordinary tale has come to light in Brownlow Hill Union, which cares for most of Liverpool's indigent. Some time ago, a little lost girl, marked with bleeding scratches from making her way through the woods, was admitted. The girl was mute but wrote her name as Olive Cobb and was known as such to all. Last week, however, upon the admission of another girl well-known to her, little Olive's speech returned, and she was able to give a proper account of herself to the Matron. Her name is Olivia Coom, (or Coomb, she is unsure of the spelling) and she used to live in Crescent Court, and for a time at Daffodil Court, Scotland Road. She is without her parents, and her next-of-kin is one Sally Coomb, but Olivia is of the opinion she may be married, and is unsure of her married name, though her husband is Hughie. They live by the Leeds & Liverpool Canal.*

Mr. Slater wrenched open the door of his study and called down the stairs to his lady.

"Mrs. Slater! Mrs. Slater! What news!"

"Grandpapa!" said Franklin, ruining out of his room. "What's the matter?"

Mrs. Slater ascended the stairs without delay, and the servants gathered in the hall, wondering what it was all about.

Mr. Slater read the piece aloud. Mrs. Slater was jubilant.

"Do you remember little Olivia Coomb?" she asked Franklin.

"Oh, yes, very well. She was here with her mother and then she went missing and everybody thought she had drowned in the canal."

They pored over the piece, marvelling that Olivia was safe and well.

"We must contact Sally Coomb—or Mrs. Henley as she is now. Do they read the newspaper, do you think? I will go to the Canal Bank today."

The Henleys did not read the newspaper, but their neighbours did, and it was not long before a man came in their back door, the newspaper in his hand.

"The little girl is alive and well!"

All were delighted.

"I will go and get her today," declared Sally. "That child shall not stay another night in the workhouse!"

"You'll 'ave to get some clothes for 'er." Mrs. Henley advised. "Ooh, 'ere's that lady again, Mrs. Slater, a-coming up the path. Very timely, I must say. Ask her for money for clothes for Olivia, Sally. I hope you don't mind but I went and sold all she 'ad, since I thought she was not coming back."

Sally did mind. She wondered, not for the first time, why she had got married in such a hurry. It was because she hated her job and had no prospects and was broken-hearted after Mr. Longman. Hughie had inferior understanding to her. She knew she would always have to think for him. But he was a hard worker and devoted to her and she knew he would always be true to her.

Sally felt embarrassed owning to Mrs. Slater that Olivia's clothes had been got rid of and that they were in need of money. Mrs. Slater, she thought, looked surprised, but said nothing and silently handed her two sovereigns.

The following morning Sally was at the porter's gate with a little bundle of clothes and was shown into his lodge to wait. He fetched Olivia, and upon the girl knowing Sally and explaining who she was, Olivia was discharged.

They walked along hand in hand. Olivia was very quiet.

"Is Mama still in America?" she asked at last.

"Your Mama is this moment on the high seas, and she'll be in Liverpool in a few days."

Olivia leaped in great jubilation. The next few days she was in a fever of anticipation, but she could not be certain that her mother was returning until she saw her coming down the gangplank at the landing stage, her Mama, yes, it was her Mama! *At last! At last!* And John and Willie by her side, much taller!

Her sobs of deep joy attracted a lot of attention at the landing-stage as passengers and crew looked fondly on at the reunion. It was the most wonderful day of Olivia's life.

# CHAPTER FORTY-TWO

**1**868

Olivia loved making confectionery. In the four years she had been employed at Chandelier Chocolates, she had learned a great deal about her craft. She had taken her mother's place in the Roasting Room, and then worked separating the beans from the hulls, but her favourite activity was enrobing, the process where the sweets were covered in an outer layer of chocolate before they went to the Packing Room.

It annoyed her that she had to add taft, the mixture of plaster of Paris and other substances to the mixture. Mr. Edward Slater had never dropped the practice, and it kept production costs down. They now had a shop on the street where they sold

Chandelier Chocolate, and it was very popular. Olivia felt embarrassed that she was associated with the adulterated confectionery.

Sometimes, she made little pieces herself out of ingredients which were left over and which she gave to the street children who always seemed to be gathered around the door.

"Mr. Slater is gone out," said Julia, glancing out the window at the middle-aged figure crossing the cobbled street. "We can relax for a while."

"Mr. Franklin is still 'ere," said Mildred. "And no doubt he will pay a visit to this room afore long," she winked at Julia, who gave a little smile. Olivia bent her head over her pan of chocolate syrup.

Franklin! He had been sent on a European Tour, and she'd only seen him once—very briefly—since he had returned. He had sent her postcards from everywhere he had stopped on his visit, to her rented room of which his father was landlord.

Mr. Edward Slater had purchased several buildings next door to each other with the view of housing his workers there. He would ensure cleanliness and dry conditions, not because he cared about them, as much as he and Jemima were fed up of sick days and workers dying from diseases contracted from the places where they lived. All workers were now required to live in Monmouth Place, and he took the rent out of their wages. It was a spartan place.

The door opened and Franklin came in as predicted. His eyes flicked momentarily to Olivia, and she returned the glance hoping none of the others saw the exchange, which they of course did.

Franklin was not very tall, but he was well-made and handsome.

"Leave your stations for a moment, I want you all in the other Pan Room." He said with a grin.

"Oh what mischief 'ave you been up to now, Mr. Franklin?" said Mildred, the oldest of the group, who felt easy bantering with the young Master.

"None at all, only I value your opinion on something new."

The followed him into the room, where he took a scoop of powdered milk from a jar, and added it to a pan of melted sugar and liquid chocolate, stirring it with vigour.

"Taste," he said with enthusiasm, after it had cooled a little. "Come on, take a spoon, before it hardens."

"Oh it is delicious!" Julia said. "Milky chocolate!"

"Powdered milk, you say? Why would anybody want to dry milk?" asked Mildred. "It'll go off, it will."

"No, not if it's done a certain way. It's very useful, for armies on the move for instance. Marco Polo used a sort of dried milk. Anyway, this is called *milk chocolate*."

"Milk chocolate! Well, I never!" Mildred said, "What do you think, Livvy?"

"It's dreamy," was the reply, a soft smile spreading over her face. "When will you begin to market it?"

"We haven't perfected the receipt yet." He smiled at her.

"You're not going to steal it from Fry's or Bourneville then?" said Olivia.

"If they had a receipt and if I had a willing spy, perhaps. But I'd prefer to develop our own secret concoction that would astound the world of chocolatiers and leave Mr. Fry and the Cadbury family with many sleepless nights."

"Milk chocolate, well I never!" said Julia, as they made their way back to the other room. Olivia lingered behind—Franklin drew closer to her, and caught her hand, pressing it.

"When may I see you? This evening, perhaps, after work?"

"This evening I go to Mama's grave to put some flowers there. It's a year ago today." A shadow crossed her face.

He pressed her hand tenderly again.

"Yes, I know. Shall I meet you at the cemetery, then?"

"Yes."

"You don't know how much I missed you when I was in Europe."

"I missed you also. Now I must go back—there is already talk."

"This evening, by your Mama's grave then. We have so much to talk of!"

If it was a strange place to meet, neither noticed. Maureen had died just one year before. She had passed away surrounded by those she loved best— her daughter Olivia and her two sons. Before she died, she had arranged apprenticeships for them, for John wanted to be a coachmaker and Willie wanted to go to sea. Olivia was happily settled in Chandelier Chocolates, having joined them at fourteen years old. The addition of another Coomb to the workforce had not been easy, but Mrs. Slater had spoken up strongly for her, and it was done. Her mother had been too ill to continue, and Olivia being taken on had meant that she could rest and try to regain her health. But it was not to be. She died at only thirty-eight years old, world-weary, and her only sorrow in leaving this world was that her children would be alone without her, especially Olivia. But she knew that Franklin Slater loved her daughter and she had confidence that Olivia would enjoy a warm family life with him someday.

Olivia missed her greatly.

The work in the factory was hard, and the hours required were long. Mr. Slater seemed to regard her as a necessary evil. His wife ignored her completely, or so she thought. Olivia was working with her old friend Julia Sullivan, who was now supporting her mother. She had urged Julia to apply for a position there. She appreciated now what Sally and Debra had endured when she was only a small child, long hours and uncomfortable conditions, all for a little money.

After she finished work that evening, she bought a bouquet of yellow roses and gypsophila from a flower stall and made her way to the cemetery, to her mother's grave. She was still greatly saddened by her loss, but if she had not Franklin's return to think about, she did not know what she would have done.

"Oh, dear Mama. I miss you so much. Every day. But I can't grudge you the happiness you have now, no I don't wish you back to a hard life like you 'ad with all the trouble and sorrows. No, rest in peace with God and the angels, Mama." She laid the flowers down, and turned to find Franklin beside her, his head bare and bowed, his hands clasped before him. She took his arm, and they left the quiet and peace of the cemetery for the busy streets.

## CHAPTER FORTY-THREE

They made their way to a little café a few streets away. There, he ordered coffee and buns.

"Won't your mother expect you home for dinner?" asked Olivia with a smile.

"I told her I would be late—that I was meeting a friend."

"Was she suspicious?"

"No, at least—I don't think so."

The coffee was brought and poured, and Olivia took a sip.

"Some experts can tell where coffee comes from by tasting it, but I can't tell where this came from, can you?"

"I think, a little shady garden in Dutch Indonesia, Sumatra to be exact, the western part."

She burst into laughter.

"Oh you are a card, you are!"

"No, I have no idea." He lowered his voice. "For all I know, this coffee might have been adulterated with dyed peas, ground. It happens, you know. Like in chocolate and sweets such as my father makes. You know what he uses. But he says everybody does it. That doesn't make it right." He looked a little glum.

"Will you continue the practice, when you get more control, I mean?"

"Oh no. My grandfather Slater talked to me a great deal about confectionery, what a fine craft it is, and the importance of using ingredients of the purest quality, and being proud of it. But what do you think of my milk chocolate idea?" he added, brighter. "Should I try it? Father, of course, will oppose me. He won't lay out the money for powdered milk. No, it's useless to even ask my father."

"You should experiment on your own, then. Perhaps someday, you'll branch out on your own."

"Father and mother will never allow it."

She finished her bun and coffee. "I'm afraid I have to go. I told Sally—my step-sister—that I'd walk out to her house this evening, as it's Mama's anniversary. And as it's Saturday, I'll stay the night."

"Sally! I remember her. I was only a boy then."

"Do you remember the first time you met me?"

"Yes, I do. I gave you stamps."

"I stuck them on the bedpost. We sold that bed. Someone else is looking at them now."

They laughed as they got up to go. "Do you still collect stamps?"

"Oh no. I gave my collection to a young chap at Eton. My fag."

They walked out together and parted with a discreet kiss.

# CHAPTER FORTY-FOUR

Sally's children saw Aunt Livvy coming along the towpath and ran to greet her. She had not forgotten to bring bonbons and they fell upon them immediately.

"Oh not before their tea, Livvy!" Sally groaned when she went inside.

"Oh sorry!" Olivia came into the living-room. "How are you?"

"I'm fine I suppose," said Sally. "There's another little stranger on the way. Sit down."

"When?"

"End of the year."

"Yours are all healthy, and this one will be too."

"I ought to thank God for that. I din't lose one of the five. Poor Hughie is 'aving to work night and day to keep us fed."

"I brought you a few cakes."

"Did you go to the grave?"

"Yes, I put flowers there."

"She was a good person, Mother was. We din't always see eye-to-eye but she tried. I was an obstinate young woman."

Sally made supper. The children were very noisy, but afterward they went out into the long summer evening to play again, all but the smallest, a little girl of two years old, who sat on her mother's lap and sucked her thumb while Sally and Olivia enjoyed a fresh cup of tea.

"Have you heard from Debra?"

"I got a letter last week. Her Hans is going out on his own. He must be a brainy type and a very 'ard worker. Maybe if they get very rich, she'll come 'ome for a visit." Sally smiled wanly.

"You never know," said Livvy, though she thought it very unlikely.

"It's funny to think," said Sally, shifting the toddler on her lap, "that we'll most likely never see each other again. She 'as four children, and she sends me a photograph every few years, and I 'ave five, and I do the same. But we'll never 'ave a cuppa together again, and the cousins will never play with each other. It's a funny life, really. My grandparents did me a great disservice, and her too. But that's my opinion. There are some that say she's lucky to be gone out of here. But that's enough doom and gloom. How are you? Is Mr. Slater as mean as ever?"

"Yes, he is as he ever was. But Sally—I must tell you something! Now, this is happy news!"

"Oh do tell me something 'appy!" Sally said, mechanically taking a knife out of young Meg's hand and shoving it away a little.

"I have a young man, and I like him, and I know he likes me."

"Ooh, now that's brightened my day! Who is he? Do I know 'im?"

"Yes, you've met him! A long time ago."

"Then who is he?"

"He's Franklin Slater. Remember now?"

Sally's face looked a little puzzled, then as understanding hit, her eyes almost popped out of her head.

"Oh no, Livvy. Not him!"

"Oh no? Why? What's wrong with 'im?"

Sally's voice rose. "What's wrong with 'im? What's wrong with 'im?"

The child got the knife again, and Sally deftly took it out of her hand and slid it out of her reach. Meg began to wail.

"Over my dead body will you see a toff. Especially not anyone from that family." said Sally, instinctively jogging the child on her knee. "Maybe you were too young to remember—Mr. Longman," she finished with contempt. "Here, Meg." She handed her a spoon, but Meg wanted the knife and continued to wail.

"I remember the name—but I don't remember what 'appened," Olivia said, wrinkling her brow.

"I'll tell you what 'appened. He courted me, and very near ruined me, and I, the innocent that I was, I was taken in and thought he meant marriage. When he realised what I was thinking, 'e was off!" Sally snapped her fingers. "Not a word, nothing. I was so broken over him I jumped into the canal out there. Hughie jumped in and saved me."

"I remember something, but I remember you in the hospital and thinking you fell in. What relation was Longman to the Slaters?"

"He was *her* nephew. *Mrs. Miser*, we called her."

"She's still called that. But Franklin's different to that Mr. Longman, Sally. He's a good man, and went away for two years to forget me, and couldn't."

"You amuse him. That's what. And 'is family will object. No, toffs don't marry the likes of us, Livvy. They marry their own, or up. Get away from him. He'll leave you, he will. He'll be off. Now you see here," she said, looking at her two-year-old. "She wants that knife because she can't 'ave it. It's the same with you and Mr. Franklin Slater. You know you can't have 'im, so you want 'im."

"It's not like that at all."

"Livvy, mark my words. This won't end well for you. I can't stop you. But remember what I said when you're alone and there's not a sight of Franklin Slater. You'll say then, *I should've listened to my sister Sally.*"

The words settled on Olivia like a cold shower of rain. Was Sally correct? Would Franklin 'be off' when he tired of her?

## CHAPTER FORTY-FIVE

Sally's words did little to frighten Olivia. She and Sally had a relationship that was more cordial than close. They were the only two Coomb women left, and they stuck together, but they were very unalike.

She met Franklin the following Tuesday after work. They went to the café. He ordered tea and currant buns. She was watching him, looking for signs that he was insincere and dishonest. She could not detect any.

"You must be hungry. Eat something, Frank, and tell me about Switzerland."

He bit into the bun and looked at her with tenderness.

"As you can see, my European Tour did not cure me of you. Perhaps I don't want to be cured," he said, reaching for her hand.

"Dear Franklin. I missed you! But I was afraid you'd meet some heiress."

He was silent.

"Oh dear, did you?" she asked.

"Oh yes, I did. But I wasn't and am still uninterested in Miss Hilda Whittle."

"Miss Hilda Whittle! You mean from Whittle's Confectionery? I'd like to know more!" Olivia felt a little upset for a moment but recovered herself.

"I knew her brother at Eton. Unfortunately, he died in a riding accident only a year ago. Miss Whittle is heiress to a large estate and a fortune. There is no entail, you see."

"I don't understand what you mean by entail."

"If an estate is entailed, it means it passes to the male heirs only; no entail means a daughter can get all. But I don't want to talk of Miss Whittle. I only mentioned her because you wanted to know."

"Oh, please tell me." Olivia wanted to know her competition.

"She was in Switzerland with her parents. Her mother took a liking to me, because she knows my mother from King George's Birthday at Eton. Mrs. Whittle is the only woman my mother has been able to discuss the Stock Market with, and they were very impressed with each other."

"The only market I know is Paddy's Market. Is Miss Whittle beautiful?"

"To some, perhaps, but not to me." He patted her hand and smiled. "How would you like to be married to a confectioner, Olivia?"

"Oh, I—I would like it very much, if it's you, that is!" A deep blush overcame her.

"To whom should I apply for your hand? Your brother John?"

"Oh, don't mind John! He'll say yes to anything that'll make me happy!"

"Well, in that case—" Franklin drew a little silver box from his pocket and opened it. Inside, nestled in blue velvet, was a sparkling midnight blue sapphire ring set in a circle of tiny twinkling diamonds.

"Is that for me?" Olivia could hardly believe it.

"Yes. It belonged to my Grandmama. She was very fond of it and gave it to me, *for the woman I was to marry*, she said."

"Dear Mrs. Slater. She was good to Mama. And to me. Bless her soul!"

He took her hand and slipped it onto her finger.

"I've never seen anything so beautiful," she said in wonder.

They left the café and walked in a little park, where they kissed out of sight of all eyes, or so they thought.

*Sally was wrong*, Olivia thought as they parted from each other a little later outside her door. *Sally was wrong. I'm getting married!*

# CHAPTER FORTY-SIX

Mr. Green had seen enough. He turned his horse and went as quickly as he could to the house in Knotty Ash and pulled the doorbell. He asked for Mrs. Slater and was shown into the drawing room.

When she heard what Mr. Green had to say, she was furious.

"Are you sure it was Miss Coomb?" she said. Upon verifying that the girl had come out of the factory and that she wore a red bonnet, she paid him and dismissed him.

Her husband came in a little later.

"Franklin is keeping company with that Coomb girl."

"You can't be serious!"

"Get rid of her, Edward. I knew she was trouble."

"I certainly will. History repeats itself. A low Coomb female goes after a Slater and must pay accordingly."

He poured himself a whiskey and water.

"On the other hand, if I dismiss her, won't that inflame Franklin? Henry ran, but Franklin is a softie. All that money spent on Eton." He sighed.

"No, he won't. Leave it to me. I will take care of Franklin."

"How? Are you going to say I will disinherit him?"

"That among other threats."

"What?"

"Never mind; you don't have to know."

She waited up for Franklin and as soon as he came in, she opened the drawing room door and asked him to step inside.

"I've had you followed." she said briskly.

"What?"

"I said that I've had you followed."

He sank down on a chair.

"Two years ago, I suspected something between you and that Coomb girl. So we sent you away. We knew the Whittles were touring Europe also and that you'd probably meet them at some point, and you did. What did you think of Miss Whittle?"

"She's all right, I suppose."

"She had better be more than all right. Because you're going to marry her."

He threw his legs out on the carpet as his eyes swivelled to the ceiling.

"That's a fantasy of yours."

"Sit up straight, Franklin. And hear me. You will marry her."

"Well I won't, and there's an end to it." He got up and made for the door.

"Come back! I did not dismiss you yet."

He paused and turned about.

"Firstly, Miss Coomb will lose her position tomorrow."

An angry cloud passed over his countenance, but then he said,

"Makes no difference, Mother, we're getting married. I gave her grandmother's ring. We're engaged. I will take care of her."

"And what will you two live on? You'll be disinherited."

"We'll start our own business. She's a dab hand at making chocolates, and I'm not too bad either."

"It's irrelevant what you will live on anyway, because you're not going to marry her. I haven't worked all my life for you to throw all this—" she threw her arm out in a general way "—away on a ragged schemer from Scotland Road. It is not going to happen, Franklin."

"Mother, might I remind you I am well over twenty-one years of age?"

"You still won't marry her. We need to increase our wealth, and the best way, the old-fashioned time-honoured way, is to marry wealth. That's why I want you to marry Miss Whittle. And now I will tell you why *you* want to marry Miss Whittle."

He gazed at her in astonishment.

"Because if you do not, your Miss Coomb will either go to prison or be transported. I will arrange it."

He was speechless.

"I don't have time to persuade and cajole and beg. I don't waste time. I have a business to run. So instead of wasting weeks or months trying to make you see sense, and then coming to this conclusion, I thought I'd let you know straightaway. I'm prepared to eliminate anybody who gets in the way of business."

Franklin found his voice at last.

"You are threatening to have her accused of a crime, to rot in prison for years perhaps?" he said at last.

"Well, yes. I am prepared to do that."

"How? How do you know a jury wouldn't acquit her?"

His mother smiled. "You know Inspector Green."

"Yes, I suppose so."

"Some years ago, we found out that he has some very bad personal habits, hidden from his wife and family, and his Chief, of course. Since we let him know that we know, he is very helpful to us. He knows about the adulteration, he knows about other matters, and he would see to it that Miss Coomb would be convicted. Now do you understand me?"

Franklin was stunned. Finally he decided to appeal to his mother's better nature, if she had any.

"Mama, I don't know why I even need to articulate the following point—Olivia is a real person. You are speaking of her as if she were a chess piece."

"Poor persons are worth very little. Why should she get in the way of my ambitions? I want to be richer, and your father and I have decided that you marrying money is the only thing to do."

"I see that I'm also a chess piece. We're pawns, Olivia and I. And yo—you are my mother," he said, in a wondering tone.

"Don't get sentimental. I'm not interested in all that silly maternal business. You know that. In any case, arranged marriages are the usual thing among the rich. Love is for shepherds and shepherdesses."

"You have an icy heart, Mother."

"Inspector Green only needs a word from me to begin this process. Or we have another plan—Mr. Standish of Northern Coal is a friend of your father's—you would not want her nieces and nephews to go hungry if her brother-in-law lost his job, would you?"

"Mother, that is unspeakable. That is pure evil."

"If it is, then evil is very common. Poor people are worth nothing to rich people like us. You see, for all my faults, I'm not a hypocrite, and I can admit it. In general, the poor are subject to us, and we get rich. But I think I've persuaded you.

You are to leave Liverpool within the hour and stay away for a month, and when you return, you will marry. We'll arrange it all, you only have to be brought to the altar. You will marry Miss Whittle."

"And don't even think of sending a message to Miss Coomb. She is quitting Monmouth Place almost as we speak. Now go."

# CHAPTER FORTY-SEVEN

The warden's footsteps clicked along the corridor, and a few girls, chatting together with excitement in Olivia's room, wondered what she wanted with them at this time of night. Perhaps they had been too noisy, but it was such a special night! Olivia was engaged to Franklin Slater! One of their own had captured the heart of the owner's son. It bode well for them all to have a friend in a position of power. They knew Olivia would not change; she'd always regard them as friends, she'd change things for the better. And if Olivia could marry up and in a true love-match at that, could not any one of them do the same? The ring was admired with delight.

Mildred was the only one who was less excited than the others. She remembered Sally and Debra and what had happened to them.

The footsteps paused outside the door, and it was flung open.

"Out, everybody. I want to speak with Miss Coomb."

The girls got up and looking wonderingly at each other, left the room. Mildred shook her head slowly as she shut the door after her.

"What's wrong?" asked Olivia in alarm.

"You've to go. Now. Pack your box, and out."

"Why?"

"Because I got a letter from Mrs. Slater saying so." She took a note from her pocket and thrust it at her.

*We have been seriously misled in her character, she must not stay another night under our protection, and needless to add, her position with Chandelier Chocolates is terminated forthwith.*

Olivia was astounded.

"There's a letter for you too," said Mrs. Cook, handing her a sealed envelope.

*Miss Coomb, I have had the most distressing interview with my son. It appears you expect to marry him. Whatever he has said, whatever he has given you, there is to be no misunderstanding, my son is already engaged. Do not try to contact him. He leaves Liverpool this evening. Jemima Slater.*

Mrs. Cook waited while, with trembling hands, Olivia took down her gowns and other garments and bundled them into her plain carpet bag. She wrapped her shawl around her and tied her bonnet beneath her chin. Her few possessions—a hairbrush, a little looking-glass, and other items were packed also. Her Bible was taken from her table. Her reticule, containing what was left of her wages, was on her arm. She was ready.

Mrs. Cook marched her down the hallway and the stairs, saw her out the front door and banged it behind her.

Olivia gulped. It would be dark soon. What would she do? Where would she go? To Sally, she supposed.

## CHAPTER FORTY-EIGHT

"**I** knew it," Sally said, letting her in, seeing her tear-streaked face. "History repeatin' itself. I did it, and was punished. You did it too, and was punished. And he's gone, isn't he?"

"They must have threatened 'im."

"Maybe, but how much love did he 'ave if he caved in so easy?"

"I don't know!" Olivia wept into her handkerchief.

"I know it's 'ard." Sally patted her shoulder. "I went through the exact same thing myself. Don't do anything stupid, now."

"I won't. Mama would hate if I did something like that. After what she went through, with the Famine, and poor Papa, an' all her troubles. She kept on."

"And don't drown your sorrows neither. That's why I jumped. I drank a bottle of gin and lost my reason. Drink is a terrible thing if you're down. So stay away from it."

"I never take anything, Sally!"

"Glad to 'ear it. Now you drink that cuppa there, and I have to put the small ones to bed. Deborah! Put that scouse on the stove for your father!"

Miserable as Olivia was, she couldn't weep opposite the children. Their welcoming smiles consoled her heart. *Auntie Livvy was staying the night again!* It was a treat they loved, even though she would hardly get a wink of sleep, with young Deborah restless in the bed beside her. Dear little ones! They didn't know yet that life could throw horrible things their way. She put on a brave face and put her broken heart aside until she could be alone, for she knew she couldn't stay here. There wasn't enough room. Or enough food.

Franklin, in spite of his mother's threats, sent a letter to Olivia, to her sister's address. It ran:

*My parents leave me with no choice. They are not only determined to punish me, but you also, and even those close to you, for our continued attachment. It's over, Olivia. I am deeply sorry. I have to marry their choice.*

After she read it, she gave it to Sally to read also.

"Humph!" was her sister's reaction. "He absolves himself of blame, doesn't 'e? Lily-livered 'e is, on top of everything."

Olivia did not want to think of Franklin like that.

"I'm sure there was some horrible threat," she said, to Sally's exasperated sigh.

"What will you do now?" she asked. "You can 'ave a home 'ere but you'll 'ave to find a job."

"I don't want to stay in Liverpool. I don't ever want to see him again. I think I'll go to London to Cousin Peg."

"Are you going to sell the ring?"

"By rights, it's supposed to belong to the woman he marries. But he's not asking for it back, is he?"

"Don't even think of giving it back! He owes you that much. And you might need it in London."

## CHAPTER FORTY-NINE

L ONDON

The first thing Olivia noticed was the noise and the rushing crowds. Everybody in England's capital seemed to be in a frightful hurry. She disembarked the train and carrying her bag, took a few moments to look around. Nobody took any notice of her; she wondered that if she fell dead on the platform, would anybody see? And what a din!

Try as she might, she could not get Franklin out of her head, and even though she stood up for him with Sally, she felt that she had been betrayed. How could he have caved in to his parents' demands so easily? Her mother's words came back to her from a long time ago.

*"It's too bad he'll end up like the rest of them."*

*"What do you mean, Mama?"*

*"Greedy. That's what I mean. They're all greedy ... maybe there are some that aren't. But the Slaters are."*

They threatened to disinherit him, and that did it. Franklin would continue to work in the business, and he would add the taft also, and take shortcuts wherever he could, and cheat people, treat his workers badly, and dismiss anybody who got in the way.

*No, Franklin can't get like that!*

She'd have to pray for him not to become mean and grasping! There was hope—his grandparents' influence. Good, kind people, the Slaters might have taught him to be honourable. But how could she think him honourable now, when he had broken faith with her? Promises! What good were promises? People made them in the heat of the moment and then, when they had time to think about them, reneged. She had long ago forgiven her mother for going to America without her, and not coming back immediately, and maturity had shown her that her mother had had no other choice. But she had not forgotten that her mother had promised and then failed to keep her promises. It was the same with Franklin. Promises were given too lightly.

Making her way from the station, she made her way to her aunt's address. It was a long walk to Spitalfields. As she neared, the hawkers and costermongers increased in number and noise. She turned a corner into a market of sorts, bustling, colourful and interesting—mongers selling old clothes and materials from shops and stalls. Her path was jammed with carts, barrows and the occasional carriage. The chatter, calling and haggling was loud in her ears. Everybody was shouting.

"Can you show me the way to Hart Street?" the first woman she asked, who had clothes draped over each arm and was proclaiming them to be *'very cheap,'* did not hear her at all, and she passed on, to a toothless old woman who pushed a faded old gown up against her before she could say anything, and told her she looked *'mighty fine, and it wor only a shilling, and if she didn't loike the blue, she 'ad one very loike in green, belonged to a Lady, they did, in Grosvenor Square.'*

When she could get a word in, she was directed around the corner, and made her escape threading her way through crowds, with the woman calling after her that she'd reduce the price to *'eleven pence hy-pny!'*

The people talked different in London.

She came to her cousin's address, which, compared to the houses adjoining it on either side, seemed well-kept, and knocked on the door. It was opened by an ancient man with a wig, in ruffled white shirt and black tails, who looked as if he had emerged from another century.

"I'm looking for Mrs. Peg Dowling, is she in, please?" asked Olivia, half-afraid of this apparition before her.

"Peg, is it? Who are you?"

"I'm her cousin, Olivia."

"Ooh. From Liverpool, is it?"

"Yes, is she in?"

"No, but here's the letter you sent." The man darted off with surprising agility and returning, gave her an unopened letter. "Sorry. I couldn't give it her. She's dead these past three months. I wor keeping' it—*in case*."

He didn't say '*in case of what*,' but London was a very strange place, and here was a very odd man, and Olivia had a sudden, fleeting thought that maybe he thought Cousin Peg might come back for her post …

but that thought was quickly overtaken by the disconcerting news.

"Dead? Mrs. Dowling is dead?" Olivia did not remember meeting Cousin Peg, ever, but it was sad to hear that she was dead.

"Yes, Miss. Would you loike to come in?"

"No, thanks. What did my cousin die from?"

"She went in her sleep. By the way, you're next-of-kin."

"Am I? How do you know?"

"Her husband is dead, they had no issue, and there's nobody else 'as called and claimed kinship. I was apprenticed to a prestigious legal firm for five years," he added with authority.

Olivia contemplated this development for a moment.

"What happened to her belongings?"

"They're all still here, Miss. I kept them—just in case."

"I see." She hesitated, thinking.

"Her room is still vacant. I hadn't the heart to clear it out and get another tenant—"

"Just in case," Olivia smiled.

"Who else lives here, besides you, Mr.—?"

"Mr. Curran, at your service, Miss. My rooms are all of them let out to ladies. And I keep a cook."

"If you're going to let out her room again, I'd be interested in taking it, perhaps."

"You had better come in and see it, then, Miss."

She took a deep breath and stepped into the hallway. It was very dark after the bright sunlight and seemed narrow and cramped full of furniture: an umbrella stand, a hall stand, trunks and chests piled one on top of another. An enormous Grandfather clock tick-ticked with solemnity.

Mr. Curran pushed open the door of the front room.

"Here it is. Mrs. Dowling's former room. Untouched since she was carried out."

Olivia hesitated a little, then feeling that she was being over-cautious, went in with what she hoped was a confident, woman-of-the-world air, looking at the cluttered room, the bed over by the corner, a fireplace with a nice mantelpiece. A table groaned under the weight of boxes piled on top, a wardrobe and a few chairs completed the furniture. The wallpaper was purple diamond patterned and the curtains were scarlet.

"That door there in the back—that goes into another room, smaller than this. So it's two rooms really, but I only let it out as one." He threw the door open. It was small and empty.

"Do you know that Peg's cousin James O'Brien stayed 'ere too, for a few months? Many years ago."

"Uncle Jimmy! I never knew he was in London at all!" She felt happy to hear it, thinking that if the landlord knew and liked her family, then she could not do better.

*I don't care for the colours,* she thought to herself, looking about the main room again, noting that the bedspread was purple also, and a red lamp was by the window.

"I'll take it," she said, making up her mind very quickly. "But I would like to meet the other ladies."

"They will be in later on," he said. "Do you have an occupation, Miss Coomb?"

"Unfortunately, not yet, Mr. Curran."

"The other ladies may be able to help you with that matter. You may find you want to fill your cousin's shoes. I shall leave you now to become settled."

He left and shut the door. Olivia sank on the bed and took off her boots, taking in the garish, saucy colour scheme of the room.

"Oh no!" she said aloud. "No! Cousin Peg! How could you! Now I know! I have to leave this place immediately! And whatever was Uncle Jimmy doing here? No, impossible. He can't have known—"

Then the front door opened, and she sprang up to peep out her door. A small group of women passed through the hall. They were all dressed alike, in long blue habits with wide sleeves, and white veils.

*Nuns!*

# CHAPTER FIFTY

The Sisters of Hope worked in the rookeries, the infamous slums near St. Giles Church. They had arrived a year ago, and so far had not secured their own building suitable for use as a convent, so they rented rooms from Mr. Curran.

She met them later and they told her about her cousin Peg. She bought and sold second-hand clothes. She was a good and charitable woman, and whatever she had to spare went to the Sisters for their work.

"Her room is in purple and red," said Olivia. "I hope to change the colours. It's far too much."

"She loved very vibrant colours," said Sr. Agatha.

"Will you take away the red lamp?" asked Sister Sarah.

"Oh, yes, I will."

"Our prayers have been answered, Sisters," beamed Sr. Mary.

Olivia unpacked and tried to make the room a home. Her treasure was her mother's jewellery box given to her by her father as a wedding present. She hung up her clothes and arranged a few decorative items on the mantelpiece. She put Uncle Jimmy's snuff box there. Her childhood treasures had long gone, it was now just a memento of her uncle.

When she had finished, she looked around. It would take quite a while for her to call this room home. She felt homesick for Liverpool already.

# CHAPTER FIFTY-ONE

L IVERPOOL

"Please don't think I want this anymore than you do," said the new Mrs. Slater. "I only agreed to it because they threatened me. You want my inheritance, and my father—"

She stopped, adjusting her veil.

"I don't want your inheritance. And your father —what?"

"My father wants to take over Chandelier Chocolates," she said. "He thinks it will be easier to persuade your parents this way."

"Indeed?" Franklin felt anger swell up inside. "I don't think he'll find it easy."

"He'll find it simpler than you think. My father is a collector. He collects companies and then he sells them off again, for all the charm, for him, is the acquiring of them."

"And you? How do you feel about it all?"

"Business is not my concern. Women are only pawns."

He was silent for a moment.

"Not just women," he said with bitterness.

"I suppose it's time for us to go down and enjoy the Wedding Breakfast," she said. "But are you going to kiss me first?"

He kissed her without emotion or passion.

"I feel exactly the same as you do," she said. "But we must do our duty. Mama explained it all to me. They will expect grandchildren."

"Hilda, was there someone else you loved?"

"Yes, there was. But it could not be. He's the fourth son and has nothing."

"I'm sorry," Franklin said. "I loved someone else too. What did they threaten you with?"

"Disinheritance. Giving it all to a cousin. But worse than that, ruining my true love."

"Maybe they thought your lover was a fortune-hunter."

"No, he loved me ever before Gerald was killed. We should go down now. They're waiting for us."

The descended the stairs hand in hand and smiled to the applause.

# CHAPTER FIFTY-TWO

**L**ONDON

Olivia had no ready cash to pay rent so she took the clothes to the market and sold them to a vendor, and those that were not sold, she gave to the Sisters for the poor, as the people who lived in the rookeries were desperately in need.

Mr. Curran repapered her room in azure blue and white, and she chose curtains to match. She was very pleased. A funny man he was, yes, but rather endearing. It was a little comfort in a strange city to have a room just the way you liked it. She'd had a letter from Sally that morning. Franklin was married, it had been in the paper, so after a little cry in her new blue room she'd had to stop and face practicalities. It was done. Franklin was out of her life forever.

And how was she to keep herself? She wondered if she could make sweets and chocolates, she knew the basics, and all she needed were ingredients and a few pieces of equipment. She asked Mr. Curran about it, and he made the helpful suggestion that she could even sell them out the window if she didn't want to hawk them about.

"I hope," he added "That you won't use any adulteration. The Adulteration Act of 1860 forbids it."

"Act or no Act, I wouldn't dream of it," she said.

"I didn't think you would, Miss. But I just thought I'd mention it—just in case."

Olivia sat down at her table under the window and wrote out the chocolate making process and what she would need.

"Oh, this involves more than I thought! I'll have to get a regular supply of cocoa beans, sugar and spices at warehouse prices. I'll have to have an oven to roast them, a cracker and fanner to get the hulls off, and then a grinder to make the powder … and pans

—what next? How to remove the cocoa butter?" She frowned, biting the end of the pencil.

*If I'm going to try this, I have to decide what kind of product I want to begin with and work backward! I can't do everything from drinking cocoa to sugared almonds. I'm not a factory with ten hands. I have to start small.*

She thought of Franklin and what they had dreamed of together and fresh tears fell on the paper. She would have to put him out of her head! And yet, she needed to think of him, to remember what they had planned, so that she would know what to do. Firstly, he would have the purest, best ingredients, according to his late grandfather's standards. Franklin had said that in the beginning, they'd do just one or two confections and when they began to make a profit, expand into others, and see what sold and what did not.

She sat back in her chair for a moment, dreaming.

They had even bandied possible names about for their business. He had wanted it to be *'Ollie's Chocolates.'* She'd wanted it to be *'Franklin Confections.'* Another had been *'Merseyside Munches.'*

Then, the bitterness returned. She's been abandoned by him. She was on her own. And her little enterprise would never be named after him.

And how to pay for the equipment she would need? She went to her mother's jewellery box. The sapphire ring sat among them like a Queen among her subjects. She took it up and looked at it, her memories tinged with sorrow. But she had no more use for this. It would have to be pawned or sold.

That night, she decided she'd make chocolate-dipped almonds.

CHAPTER FIFTY-THREE

"**I** know exactly the man to 'elp you," Mr. Curran said brightly. "He's the son of an old friend of mine, name of Lionel Brandon, a businessman who runs a beer-house just a few streets away."

Olivia was not sure how the landlord of *The Eleventh Hour* could help her, but Mr. Curran assured her that he knew everybody.

That evening, after supper, Mr. Brandon called. He was a spare-built man, handsome in a quaint sort of way, and though several years her senior, she felt a little attracted to him. He hadn't much time to spare, he said, as his boy was looking after the customers.

Olivia quickly outlined what she needed. Yes, he could help her. He knew where to make enquiries. A woman going into business, and on her own! He raised an amused, but disapproving, eyebrow.

"I will pay for all of it myself, of course," she said.

"You can afford to?"

"Yes, tell me the price, and I'll get the money."

"You must've found a fortune left by the late Mrs. Dowling," said Mr. Brandon. Olivia thought that was rather rude and did not reply.

"Perhaps if you could purchase the cocoa beans already roasted and hulled and even ground to powder, you would not have to lay out a great deal of money on equipment until you saw how sales were," he very sensibly said after a time. She thought that was a good idea. Also, she could begin at what was her favourite part—panning, enrobing, and packing the sweets into pretty little gold and silver paper bags. In the end, all she might need was a large pan or two and paper. She could make the bags herself.

Two days later, he was back. He had good news— he'd negotiated with a confectionery factory owner who wanted rid of his shop, but wanted to carry on the manufacturing side. He was willing to accomplish the first part and sell her the roasted, hulled, and powdered cocoa beans.

"I will be sold beans that are 100% beans?" she asked Mr. Brandon, with firmness.

"Of course!"

"Because I won't accept chicory or dyed peas among them. I can tell if there is adulteration. I have to use the purest ingredients."

"I shall ensure that there's no adulteration," he said. "In fact, if you were to come with me to this factory, I would be very pleased; then you can tell Mr. Wilson this yourself."

"Very well," she said, pleased.

They set out the following day, taking a cab. On the way, Mr. Brandon made good conversation, was very particular about handing her down, and made sure she avoided a puddle. He offered his arm.

It was exciting to be in a sweet factory again, although the scents and sights brought back memories of Franklin. She met Mr. Wilson. He seemed a pleasant, reliable man and she left, reassured that all would be well. Mr. Brandon saw her to her door, again handed her down, and then kissed her hand. She thought it impertinent, but Mr.

Brandon's attentions reached a place in her heart that felt lonely, aching and hopeless.

Over the next few weeks, as he oversaw the start of her business, and brought her ledgers and other necessities for account keeping, she began to depend upon him more and more. Her first confections were a great success. She took Mr. Curran's advice and opened the sash window and sold them to people passing by, four for a penny. The summer passed quickly and by autumn, she was making a tidy sum and Mr. Brandon asked her to marry him, promising that if she did, she could have proper tea-rooms, on his premises, and could have a staff of her own to run it.

He asked her to think about it.

She was in a quandary, and wished she had a friend to talk the matter over with. She missed Julia and Mildred—they'd have been able to advise her.

The nuns had moved into their own convent, and a family had moved in upstairs. A happy, noisy family whose laughter and singing reached her in the evenings, and it made her loneliness even worse. She longed to be a part of a family again. She wanted a husband and children.

She accepted Mr. Brandon's proposal. What did she have to lose, she wondered? Though she could not ever love him like she loved Franklin, he was dead to her. As good as dead.

She could love Brandon more and more as time went on.

# CHAPTER FIFTY-FOUR

L IVERPOOL

The first inkling of trouble for Mr. and Mrs. Edward Slater was when they read in the newspaper that Inspector Green was removed from his position for suspected corruption and witness intimidation.

"Is there anything they could find that would damage us, Edward?" asked Mrs. Slater in her drawing room that evening as she opened a ledger.

"Not much, but what a fool he was to write things down anywhere! He's the least of our troubles, Jemima."

"What do you talk of?" Mrs. Slater looked up.

"Our esteemed in-laws wish to purchase our business."

'What? Does Whittle think we want to sell, is that it?"

"No, he does not. He wants to have a monopoly in this town—indeed in all Lancashire."

"I hope you said 'no' to that."

"Of course, and then he said we would *have* to sell soon."

"What are you saying?"

"He said we'll go bankrupt."

"That is utterly ridiculous!"

"He will undercut us, ruin us."

"Our own son's father-in-law!"

"He offered a good sum for the Company, more than it's worth, in fact."

"More than it's worth! Then take it! We'll invest the money elsewhere! We can get involved in cotton manufacture, but production is getting too expensive, with public opinion against child labour. Schools for the poor, indeed! I think a move away from England would do us good. Perhaps Kentucky or Georgia. I imagine ex-slaves will work for next to nothing. Or we can go to India or Brazil. It would also take us away from any unpleasantness that could emerge as a result of Green's arrest. Oh, find out where we can make the most return for the smallest investment!"

"I shall act without delay, then. Jemima."

"We shall leave Franklin to his mercy. And his wife. Oh, I quite forgot to tell you, Edward. He told me last week that a child is expected."

"Do you wish to stay until the child is born, Jemima?"

"What for? You know I don't like children. If I'd had any choice in the matter, I would not have had *any*."

"We need a lot of capital to start again," Edward stroked his beard. "As much as we can get."

## CHAPTER FIFTY-FIVE

ONDON

Mr. Brandon had two houses. The public house was on the corner of Brickly Street and Love Lane. Its name, *The Eleventh Hour,* was emblazoned above the door in large bronze letters. His private apartments were upstairs. The house beside it, on Brickly Street, was let in rooms.

Before she married, Mr. Curran asked her if she was sure this was what she wanted. He had not thought that this introduction would lead to marriage. Not that there was anything wrong with marriage, he was all for it. But some people said that his son's friend was a *dark horse.* He was sorry to speak so, but she had no father to advise her.

"It's kind of you, Mr. Curran. But Mr. Brandon is so attentive to me, and so kind, he has won his way to my heart."

"Very well, then. But I won't let your room until you've come down the aisle, just in case."

His attitude caused her a little concern, but when she told Lionel about it later, he laughed.

"Did he tell you about Miss Tremblay also?"

"Miss Tremblay? No—who is Miss Tremblay?"

"She was a friend long ago. An actress. I have not seen her for five years and I will not see her for five or ten more; it's immaterial to me."

"Where is she?"

"I don't know. Edinburgh, Dublin. It's irrelevant."

"But you do love me, Lionel, don't you?"

"Why are you asking me such a question? I'm giving you an establishment, both domestic and for business."

He would not say he loved her, but Olivia thought that he was just the kind of man who found it difficult to talk of his feelings. The license was obtained, and they were married in a quiet ceremony, and she moved into the apartments above his pub. There was to be no wedding journey, he had not time for that, whenever he left his business to others, he said, he was cheated.

Olivia had not been married three months when she came to the realisation that she had acted hastily. Her husband had a cold heart and wanted to control everything she did, even in her own business. He also had an evil temper.

She saw this one day when the boy spilled beer over a man's coat. It had not been poor Charlie's fault—the customer had jerked back suddenly when Charlie had been just behind him.

"How dare you!" Mr. Brandon had grabbed the boy's ear and flung him toward a table. "Be more careful in future!" he bellowed. "There's a queue of boys waiting to get in here to work, and one of these days I'll kick you out."

"Yes, guv'nor. Sorry, sir." Charlie pulled himself up, shaking, rubbing his ear.

When she got an opportunity, she asked Lionel why he had not been more patient with Charlie.

"I saw what happened. It wasn't his fault," she explained, over their hurried lunch in the back parlour.

"Olivia, let us make one thing clear between us. I will manage my own staff."

"But poor Charlie—he's only fourteen—and he's supporting his family. They are eight in number. What's the matter, Lionel? Why do you look at me like that?"

"Because you did not hear me when I told you not to interfere. My staff is my affair. Never do that again." He dug his fork into his pie.

"But Lionel, I only—"

"Be quiet!" he shouted. "Did you not hear me? If we are to live in harmony, Mrs. Brandon, you cannot question me. Ever."

There was a dreadful silence. He ate noisily, banging his utensils, in deep anger.

Olivia got up and ran upstairs to their bedroom, where she flung herself on the bed and cried. She waited for him to come up and make peace, but he did not. That evening, he did not address her at all. It was as if she was not there. The following day brought no change. He spoke to her only when necessary. When she begged him, on the third day, to speak to her, he looked at her with coldness.

"I had thought you were a different sort of woman. But I should have known that a woman of business would be a nagging shrew. I was perhaps taken in by your youth and a little beauty. If we are to be happy, you must learn. Never question me in my business, my friends and associates, or anything."

Frightened by his coldness, she only said:

"I thought you were a kind, caring man."

"I do not know where you got that idea from. Because I helped you, I suppose. Because I gave you a Tea Room. Which is where you should be now, instead of causing trouble between us."

She withdrew without replying.

She thought briefly of Franklin—oh why was he lost to her! Franklin would never, ever have treated her like that! As she lay with her husband that night, she thought of Franklin again—would he treat her in this silent, unloving way? No! What a lucky woman Miss Whittle was, to be Mrs. Franklin Slater now!

*Stop thinking of Franklin!* She said to herself, almost in despair. *He betrayed you!*

When Lionel went to sleep, she sobbed silently.

She was destined to be unhappy for the rest of her life. Or would she get used to his cold and distant nature? Would she become cold and distant herself, unable to love?

But there was always hope he would improve. In time, he could grow to love her. And then it would be better. Perhaps she just had to be patient.

# CHAPTER FIFTY-SIX

Christmas brought jollity to the East End, there was merriment and goodwill, carol-singing and lights and even Lionel was in better humour. Olivia wondered if 1869 would bring her happiness.

On Christmas Day, he apologised for his ill-humour and said that he hoped she could forgive him.

"I'm selfish, I know that," he admitted. She flung her arms about him and he kissed her.

*Everything will be well from now on!* She thought happily. All we need is time to get used to each other. If we are patient, we can be happy and content.

On the first Sunday of the year, they had a good dinner at one o'clock. The pub was closed.

"You have turned this house into a home," he said to Olivia, and her heart soared. He sat by the fire and lit a cigar, smiling.

There was a knock on the street door. Annie, their servant, went down to open it, and Olivia heard a female voice.

She thought it was Mrs. Kelly who lived next door who had promised her a pudding, and she got up to speak to her downstairs as she was elderly and wanted to spare her the stairs.

But to her great surprise, it was a tall woman approaching middle-age, in rich coral velvets and white furs, with a very elaborate hat of nests and fruits and feathers, who was hurrying up the stairs. Barely giving her a glance, she swished past her, crying out:

"Lionel! Lionel! Guess who!"

Annie was pale and wringing her hands. Olivia darted up after the woman, who had now burst in upon Lionel with cries of delight. She was just in time to see her fling herself at Lionel, who had stood up, and cry out,

"Brandon, you bad, bad boy! Why have you not written to your dear Cecile? Did you think I would not come back to you? You silly man! But you must have been expecting me—everything looks so nice! Who let my secret out? Who?" she touched his nose with her white-gloved finger.

Lionel looked as if he had been shot. Olivia had entered the room, and the woman looked around. She was a handsome woman, whose beauty had worn well, though she had help from powder and rouge.

"Who is this? I passed you on the stairs, did I not? My apologies. You must be a relative of Lionel's. If I had known, I would have acted and spoken with more decorum! You must be his niece!"

Her countenance altered as in the ensuing silence she took in the true situation.

"Cecile, allow me to introduce my wife Olivia," said Lionel, in a strained voice.

"Your wife? Lionel, you got married?" she disengaged herself from him and took a step backwards. He looked like a thief whose hand had been caught in the till.

"So, you are Mrs. Brandon." The visitor had begun to tiptoe around Olivia, like a cat circles another, intruding feline. Olivia felt herself scrutinised.

"So, you found yourself a young maiden," sneered Miss Tremblay. "I hope she was worth it."

Olivia gasped and cast a glance at Lionel. It was his place to put a stop to this! But he said nothing.

"From the country too, I would bet," she went on. "Provincial. Let me hear you speak, if you can, and then I shall surely know."

Olivia's eyes filled. Lionel still said nothing.

"Oh dearie me, tears." Miss Tremblay drew her scarlet lips together in a pout. "It looks as if I'm not welcome here, nobody has asked me to sit down, or offered me a drink, so I shall take my leave."

In utter silence, she swept to the door, leaving a heavy, exotic scent in her wake.

# CHAPTER FIFTY-SEVEN

Olivia sat on the edge of a chair.

"Speak to me, Lionel. I know she's Miss Tremblay, and I know there was an intimacy between you."

He did not reply, except to turn from her and mutter half to himself: "I have made a big mistake."

He got up and left the room, the house. She was alone with the Christmas decorations, the tree, the aroma of his cigar, hints of her lingering perfume, her bitter thoughts and feelings, and her tears.

"Annie," she said to the servant when she came in with tea "Do you know much about that woman, Miss Tremblay?"

"It's not for me to say anything, Mrs. Brandon."

"But I need to know. Did she live here?"

"Oh yes, Mrs. Brandon. She lived here, and her girls too."

"Her daughters? She has children?"

"No, Mrs. Brandon. The girls working for her. I wasn't sorry to see 'em go, the lot of 'em. This was always a respectable house until he—" she stopped and left the room.

Lionel returned early the following morning, and did not wish to talk. He refused to say where he had been. In the morning he opened his premises again and ate lunch with her in silence.

"I heard you say you had made a mistake?" she said bitterly to him early the following morning when he had come upstairs about three o'clock. She was sitting up, trying to read, but she could not concentrate on her book.

"I'm going out now, and don't ask me where I'm going, cos it's none of your business," was his reply.

"It is my business! I'm your wife. You made vows to me. Don't vows mean anything? Are you going to see her?"

"I told you before, don't oppose me."

The quarrel became loud and ended in violence. Before Olivia knew it, she was spinning toward the hearthstone, and her forehead hit it with force before she fell, almost senseless, upon the fireirons. She remembered no more.

# CHAPTER FIFTY-EIGHT

She awoke in hospital. She remembered another time, long ago, when she had awoken in a hospital. She had been a little girl then.

There was something on her face. A sticky, throbbing mess. She raised her hand to touch it. A thick gauze dressing covered one side of her face. Her brow was afire with pain.

She could not recall why she was here. She thought she was in Liverpool for a few minutes. But no, this was London.

A nurse passed by the end of her bed.

"What am I doing here?" she wanted to ask, raising herself up, but no words, only a strange, unintelligible sound came from her mouth. But the nurse, seeing her awake, paused.

"How are you, Mrs. Brandon? You received two cuts to your face. The surgeon sutured them up. You have twenty stitches on the larger one, and twelve on the smaller, by your eye. And a mighty bruise on your forehead."

She sank back on her pillow. She could not remember anything. There was a quarrel with somebody—her husband—an ugly, loud quarrel, and he had grabbed her wrist and flung her away.

The doctor came and he and a nurse changed the dressings. It was very painful. The nurse cleaned her wounds with a stinging solution, and it was very difficult to bear. She moaned, but no other words came.

They asked her questions that she tried to answer, but her words were frozen within her, just as they had been many years ago. She made a sign, however, with her hands, that she wanted a mirror.

"No, not yet. Wait for them to get a little better." The nurse laid a fresh dressing on her face and expertly bound it in place. "You're lucky you still have your eye, you know."

They gave her something to help her to sleep. The next time she woke, she recognised Annie by the bed.

"How are you, Ma'am? Me and Charlie brought you in. You was unconscious. They're bad wounds you 'ave. I cleaned up the hearthrug as best I could, because you lost a lot of blood."

Again, she tried to talk, but it was impossible. She made signals for a pencil and something to write on, and Annie went out and came back with both.

*Where is Mr. Brandon?* she wrote.

"In jail, Ma'am. We called the police, you see, and they followed him to—that woman's—'otel, and they arrested him there. Now don't you fret, Mrs. Brandon. I'll look after you when you get 'ome. I'm sure a constable will be coming to see you soon. You must tell him all you remember."

*Please call to the Sisters of Hope in Denmark Road. Ask Sr. Sarah if she could come to see me.*

Annie did as requested, and Sisters Sarah and Agatha came to see her, bringing her apples and a bottle of blackberry cordial. They seemed distressed at her appearance and told her that if she needed shelter when she was discharged she could stay with them for a few days.

*Please pray for me,* Olivia wrote. She could not speak; only strange sounds came.

The constable came and interviewed her, and she was truthful, not trying to shield her husband in any way. She knew that she and Lionel would have to separate.

"Your husband says that you went for him with your scissors, and that he acted in self-defence," said the policeman.

*I can't remember exactly what happened.*

"Were you imbibing that night?"

*No. I don't drink.*

"You don't? And you live at *The Eleventh Hour?*"

*Never have drank.*

After her stitches were removed four days later, she went to the Sisters for a while, until her wound healed. But the injury to her face was nothing to the injury to her heart. If only there was a dressing for that! They tended her very well, and on the day the dressing came off, she asked for a mirror.

"Oh dear, we do not have such things in a convent, you know!" Perhaps it was a little fib, but she'd have to wait until she got home to see herself in the mirror. She left that afternoon, taking a hackney. It felt odd to be back again at *The Eleventh Hour*. It did not feel like home at all. She went straight to her bedroom to see herself in the dressing table mirror.

She burst into tears when she saw the large, raw red wound cutting across her cheek almost from her mouth, arcing up toward her ear. It was horrible indeed, and gave her a sort of one-sided grin, like the Joker in a pack of cards. She looked evil, grotesque. The other one, by her eye, was not as marked, but it too made her look horrid. A large bruise was barely visible on her forehead. She still suffered from bad headaches.

*'Oh God,'* she sobbed. *'I have to find something to thank You for, don't I? Thank you I still have both eyes! But why can't I speak?'*

She could never be seen barefaced in public again. She asked Annie—thank Heaven Annie could read well!—to go out and buy her a yard of black netting, closely woven, and set to work that very evening making herself two veils, which she weighted here and there with small black diamond-shaped stones, so that not even in a wind would it be possible for it to lift up and expose her.

"It's a beautiful veil, Ma'am." Annie tried to console her.

The pub was being managed by Mr. Stern, who came up to see her about several matters that needed attention, and for money. She did not want to see him, but he said it was urgent. She covered herself before he entered the room. He looked at her very curiously, and was astonished when she started writing her answers. He declared sullenly that neither he nor the staff had been paid since last Quarter, and when would Mr. Brandon be back? Everybody was grumbling and threatening to quit work. It was all he could do to keep them at it.

*I don't have money,* she wrote. He was angry and banged the door after him.

Alone that evening, the shock of her new situation began to hit Olivia. She acknowledged that she had not known Mr. Brandon's character at all when they had married, and she had married a brute.

*Franklin.* Again, she had to stop herself thinking of him, and remind herself that he had betrayed her.

At least Lionel was in jail, so she could stay here for a short time. But not too long—he could be released anytime. She did not know anything about law. Perhaps Mr. Curran could enlighten her.

That night, she dreamed of the workhouse, and the time when she was Olive Cobb, mute little Olive Cobb. She strongly wanted to be Olive Cobb again, or anybody but Olivia Brandon. Waking in the dead of night with the vicious pain in her head, she became afraid. Afraid that Lionel would break out of jail and harm her. She never wanted to see Lionel Brandon again.

Hiding from Lionel, and having to hide her face for the rest of her days would mean she had to become almost a different person ... would she regain her power of speech? A deeply distressing event had put her into this state as a child, and now it had happened again. She wondered what would take her out of it this time, what comfort or joy could she possibly find that would restore her?

Olivia Brandon was no more, but she was saddled with his name for good.

# CHAPTER FIFTY-NINE

O livia slowly adjusted to her new life. She was still mute, except for odd, other-world sounds that she was sure frightened people—they frightened her—so soon she stopped even trying to speak. She wrote or made signs.

She made her way back to Hart Street to Mr. Curran. It was very embarrassing to go back with her veil in place, and have to explain, in a notebook, who she was. She carried a notebook and pencil with her always.

"Oh dear, I let the room out, after your wedding, you know! But then the tenant left before Christmas, and another man came to look at it, but 'e did not like the wallpaper, and so I decided not to redecorate it, just for him—just in case—and you see, it is free again. I would be 'appy to let it to you again, Miss Coo— Mrs. Brandon."

To Olivia, it felt like coming home, and she unpacked her belongings there the very next day. Everything was placed where it was before. She had her equipment moved as well. Thankfully because Mr. Wilson was still supplying her with powdered cocoa, she had not very much.

She wrote to Lionel's attorney outlining the financial situation to him. He came to see her and informed her that Lionel was not as yet in a position to pay the tradesmen who were banging on the door or the workers in *The Eleventh Hour*. She, on the other hand, managed to pay the two girls working for her in the tea room and the little room behind where the chocolates were made.

"He has a lot of enemies," said Mr. Tarrant. "There are many creditors, some of them criminals in London's underworld. He owes a great deal of money. The Bank may seize the property and everything in it any day now. Are you going to press charges for your injuries? He said it was an accident."

The shame of having to go to Court and show her face made her shake her head. As her husband he would be expected to keep her, but she did not want anything from him.

She paid Annie and young Charlie in clothes that Brandon had provided for her. They could sell them.

One morning, Mr. Curran was out, and there was a knock at the door. The servant Jane answered, and immediately showed 'Mr. Lionel Brandon, Ma'am' into her room.

She was unveiled and turned her back immediately. She put her hands over her face, he came around her, took them away, and stared. Then he turned around and walked out. He was obviously disgusted, but the fear she had that he would demand she return to him faded away. She was surely safe from him now.

She began to go out and about more with her veil on, to become used to stares and children pointing. She'd have to hold her head up high and try not to mind. She remembered that other isolated time in her life when she had been mute. Then, God had been her best friend, God it was to whom she had poured out her silent words. It was the same now.

Some days later, Mr. Curran knocked on her door after he had come back from an early morning visit to the market.

His voice seemed agitated. "Mrs. Brandon. Bad news. May I enter?"

Thankfully, she was up. With an attitude of drama, Mr. Curran pronounced: "I'm very much afeard, Mrs. Brandon, that it is your estranged husband. Mr. Lionel Brandon was found dead of a stab wound, I believe, just outside his premises, by persons unknown. The word 'FAITHLESS' was scrawled upon the door in large black letters. The police are everywhere just now—I expect they will come here."

Dead! Lionel dead! Murdered! She sat in shock and veiled herself hastily lest the police come.

They came within the hour.

The police doubted that this wronged wife, scarred and mute, had anything to do with it, unless she hired a strong man, and Mr. Curran did not fit that category. And since there was no evidence, they left —at least for now.

She was a widow. She wondered if Miss Tremblay had killed him. *FAITHLESS!* A woman's crime.

## CHAPTER SIXTY

LONDON

"Hilda, please tell me what to do now."

"There's nothing you can do, Franklin. Nature will take its course. I don't know what to expect, but I believe it's absolutely horrid."

"Let me send a message to your father to tell him it's your time."

"No. He is probably in bed already, leave him until the baby comes. Don't tell Father—he's too upset after losing Mama, and so unexpectedly—"

Her sudden cry startled him. The midwife came to the bed, a bustling, bossy woman with a red face, and told him to wait downstairs.

"Good luck, Hilda." He kissed her moist forehead as the pain abated.

"Franklin? We try, don't we?"

"Yes, we try."

"But how miserable we are!" she exclaimed then.

"No, I'm not miserable," Franklin said before he realised that she was speaking more of herself.

She wished that *he* was not here, but that Percy was. Percy, the love of her life, denied to her by her father. As Olivia had been denied to him.

The odd thing was that he and Hilda had become friends. She'd talked to him of Percy and he had told her all about Olivia. They felt sorry for themselves and they felt sorry for each other.

Maybe they could be happy in time. They did not dislike each other. They did not quarrel. She was never jealous, nor was he.

"Mr. Slater, if you would wait downstairs, *please,*" said the midwife in an impatient voice.

He let go of Hilda's hand.

"Will it take long?" he asked the midwife.

"Oh, many hours yet."

The evening wore into night; he dozed in an armchair, and dawn crept over the neighbourhood. Franklin went upstairs at intervals.

"She's all right, and no, you can't see her," the midwife said at the door every time he appeared. "You're interrupting. Husbands get in the way."

"Should I get the doctor? It seems awfully long," he said.

"No, it's her first; of course, it's long!"

But when her maid got up, and went in to her mistress, she came running down immediately to tell him that while she didn't know much about childbirth, his wife looked very ill indeed, and that furthermore, the midwife was drunk. Franklin sprang from his chair and told the maid to send the carriage immediately for the doctor.

He sprinted upstairs and into the room, and found Hilda barely conscious, her lips dry, her skin cold and clammy. She did not seem to know him.

The midwife was dozing, an empty gin bottle by her side. He pulled her up, slapped her face, and told her to get out. She lumbered off, muttering that first babies always take a long time and what harm was a little drink to pass the time?

"Hang on, old girl. Hang on, the doctor's coming. You'll be fine, it will all be over soon, I promise." But she did not seem to hear. Then a kerfuffle downstairs announced the doctor's arrival, and he came into the room and sent him out.

Franklin fell to his knees on the landing and prayed as he had never prayed before. He was distraught. Within five minutes he heard the cry of a baby and hovered by the door, not wanting to open it, in case he disturbed the doctor and the maid who was assisting him.

After what seemed like a long time, the door opened. The doctor stood there, his sleeves rolled up, and he was wiping his hands on a towel. Franklin could hear the sound of weeping, and for a moment did not take it in.

"I'm very sorry, Mr. Slater. Your wife was drawing her last breaths as I entered the room. I delivered the child immediately, but my efforts were too late. She died as soon as the child was born. I could not save her. The child lives and appears to be healthy."

Franklin would never forget the rest of that day. He said goodbye to poor Hilda. Her maid had washed her and combed her hair and she looked beautiful in death. Franklin's tears flowed.

He was shown the child. Poor motherless little girl, wrapped up in a warm blanket, mewling, chewing her fists, already hungry for milk. The wet-nurse was sent for—Hilda had already decided that she could not feed the child herself. Did she have a premonition?

A message had to be sent to Mr. Whittle, and Franklin would never forget the grief and rage of the old man when he arrived.

"You're to blame for this," he stormed. "Why could you not see the midwife was stewed out of her senses? You, and you alone, are to blame for my daughter's death! I could shoot you this moment! Get out of this house. Get out tonight. It's not your house and I want nothing to do with you ever again. I have been truly deceived in you Slaters! Your parents gone to Brazil, having cheated me! I will take *you* for every penny you have."

"You did not care about Hilda enough to allow her to marry the man she loved, did you?"

"How dare you! Our family have always had arranged marriages! But in this case, I *did* blunder. Oh, I did indeed. How I wish I had allowed her her own way! Now I have to arrange her funeral!"

Franklin opened his mouth to speak, but his father-in-law got in before him.

"And as for the child upstairs," Mr. Whittle went on. "I never want to lay eyes upon it. That child was the cause of my daughter's death! I wish it had died! Let it be taken to the Foundling Hospital!"

"The child is none of your business, Mr. Whittle," said Franklin crisply, and quickly, before another volley from the distraught, angry man. "That is my daughter. My little girl. You have no say in the matter, nor is it your duty to arrange Hilda's funeral. She's my wife."

# CHAPTER SIXTY-ONE

Franklin left the house that evening and found rooms in a cheap hotel. The nurse had gone to her own home with the baby. She had a baby of her own.

What a catastrophe to lose Hilda! He mourned her and was utterly grateful to her for the gift of a little child. How dreadful it was that a woman should have to risk her very life bringing a child into the world.

He had held the baby and felt a great pride and affection wash over him. His child. He felt overwhelmed at the responsibility before him.

He would name her Olivia. He was sure Hilda would understand.

He felt dreadfully guilty that he had not known the midwife was drunk and neglectful. Her father was right to blame him on that account, but he knew nothing of childbirth and midwives and women's affairs. It seemed obscene to him that any nurse or midwife should betray a sacred trust by neglecting a patient.

He wished his parents back. Though hard and unfeeling in many respects, they were his parents and he longed to speak with them. But they were no more, and had left a trail of economic destruction after them. They would never return to Liverpool, or to England.

His parents had promised to sell Chandelier Chocolates to Mr. Whittle, but asked for the money in cash. The necessary papers were signed, and the cash was handed over one Tuesday evening in Knotty Ash by Mr. Whittle's lawyer, and the keys and deeds of the factory were supposed to be handed to him.

"I'm afraid I left them in the factory," Mr. Slater told Ponsonby. "Very remiss of me of course, but I shall have them delivered to your office first thing in the morning."

"Mind that you do," said Ponsonby. "If they are not there by eleven o'clock, I shall come and fetch them."

The following morning, Ponsonby hurried to the factory at eleven o' clock, and encountered Mr. Speight, a local merchant, walking about the premises as if he owned it. Questions ensued. Mr. Speight had the keys, and the deeds, and the papers were in order—signed three days before. He was the new owner and was utterly astounded that Mr. Slater had apparently 'resold' his business to Whittle Confectioners.

The Slaters were already clear of English waters, having embarked on a speedy yacht to Lisbon. After that, nobody knew where they had gone until they had sent Franklin a letter.

*Dear Franklin, we are sailing for South America tomorrow. We are starting afresh in Brazil, but as to what we shall do, we do not know. A coffee plantation perhaps, or tobacco. We wish to extend an invitation to you and to Hilda and your child to join us there. We hope Hilda will forgive us, and her father too, but business is business. We look forward to your reply. Write to us c/o Cunard, Water Street. Your loving parents.*

Betrayal! It had been very difficult as he was the only Slater left to blame. He had endured hours of questioning from the police. But as he had no shares and was not privy to any of his father's business, he was allowed to go home. Hilda had been very distressed but believed him. She had not held this crime against Franklin. She knew he was allowed no part in Mr. Slater's affairs. Her father, having nobody else to rain abuse upon (Ponsonby having been dismissed from his Firm) chose to blame his son-in-law. He blamed the Slater family for the sudden death of his wife.

It was no comfort to Mr. Whittle to find out that the ship the Slaters had boarded had gone down in mid-Atlantic with all hands. And all cash too. Reluctant to strip the young Mr. Slater of all he had because of Hilda, he had held off until now, but Franklin knew that he would now lose everything he owned.

# CHAPTER SIXTY-TWO

Franklin sold everything he could lay his hands on before his father-in-law took it. He had to pay his lodgings and Molly, the nurse. The baby was thriving, and he resolved to keep her with Molly no matter what happened. Olivia was a bright, smiling little girl who knew her Papa now and crowed in delight, waving her arms and kicking her legs when he visited Molly's cottage.

He had to find work soon. He applied to several places he knew, but the Slater name was mud in Liverpool. He tried to get a job with the father of one of his old friends from Eton, but on the day of the interview he received a message from Molly to say that Olivia was ill with fever and he hurried there instead. When he tried to set up a second interview, he was unsuccessful.

*I will do better outside Liverpool,* he thought to himself. *I'll try my luck in London. But what am I to do with Little Miss Livvy? I don't want to leave her here.*

Olivia was the most precious child in the world. If he waited just some months more the baby could be partially weaned, according to Molly. Franklin had an idea. Powdered milk instead of mother's milk?

But even if he solved the feeding problem, somebody would have to mind her while he worked.

He remembered then Mrs. Knowles, his old nurse. Would she be willing to come out of retirement and for a year or two at least, go with him and Olivia to London?

He wrote to her, and she replied a few days later. She regretfully had to decline, because of a bad leg, but she had a sister younger by ten years. Mrs. Redding would be happy to oblige. She sent on references. She had worked as a nurse in a stately house in Devonshire, and the family was now grown up, but she did not wish to retire just yet. A few years would suit her very well. She lived close to London in St.

Albans and would join him there as soon as she received his summons.

It was done! Franklin was ready to move.

# CHAPTER SIXTY-THREE

"I've heard something about powdered milk being developed for infant feeding," said Dr. Simpson. "But it's very early days. There are obvious problems with it. Firstly, hygiene. The strictest hygienic practises would have to be maintained. Cool, boiled water only. Second, the ratio of powder to water for infant feeding is not known. Too much could be as bad as too little. However, this child, at five months, can now take solid food. I'm not an advocate of pap, Mr. Slater."

"What's on earth is pap?" asked Franklin, dandling the child on his knee. "It sounds disgusting."

"Bread and milk slop. My wife fed our child from our own plate, whatever we were having, she made a mush of it and fed the baby a few spoonfuls. No salt of course. No spices, very little sugar. Plain food. Off to London, are you?"

"I have a friend who lives in Ealing. He's willing to put me up for a while, until we can get settled. His wife will help me with Olivia."

"I wish you luck then. No, no need to pay. I was saddened to hear that your father-in-law has acted in such a punitive way. Your wife's death was not your fault. If only Mrs. Slater, God rest her soul, had come to me for a recommendation, I could have sent her a first-class midwife, trained too."

Frank left the surgery, and the following day boarded the train for London, accompanied by a nurse hired for the journey, Olivia wrapped in her arms. He had compassionate glances from fellow passengers who could see, from the difference in rank between the two adults, that he was the father of a motherless child. He carried a bottle carefully prepared for Olivia and the nurse fed her when she cried.

Arriving in London, he said goodbye to the nurse, who was going straight back to Liverpool. He took a cab to Ealing, only to find that the fire engines were busy in the neighbourhood. A house had caught fire, and the house each side of it was blackened with smoke and dangerous to go into. One of the houses belonged to Mr. and Mrs. Grant. They could do nothing for him, as they had to find accommodation for themselves.

Bitterly disappointed, and hardly knowing where he was going, Franklin turned for the City. He had to be very sparing with his money, and his home would have to be very simple.

*Find lodgings, send the address to Mrs. Redding, and ask her to come as soon as she can.*

# CHAPTER SIXTY-FOUR

Olivia had her little business up and running. She employed Charlie from the pub to do the selling at the window. He was cheery and cheeky, and the customers loved him, especially the children.

"I say, guv'nor, what can I do for you? Chocolate-covered almonds, these are, four a penny, 'ere you are."

"*Ollie's Chocolates*," exclaimed the young man.

"Yeah, Ollie's Chocolates. I say guv'nor, what you doin'? Me Ma says, don't give a basin of gravy a nut, they got no teeth."

Olivia came out from the back room which she used for storage, having heard the one-sided conversation. The customer had gone on his way.

"He let 'im lick the chocolate off the nut," said Charlie. "You don't often see a bloke carrying' a basin of gravy around town, do you? Nice clobber, not from 'ere. A basin of gravy, it's a *baby, innit!*" He explained to a bemused Olivia.

She wished she could respond. She wished she could shake off this inexplicable disorder she had, that of being unable to speak. It was the frozen lake all over again. There was a kind of numbness within her. She felt impatient with herself, and sad. She wasn't Olivia anymore. She was someone else now. A scarred, veiled lady, and a widow under suspicion of murdering her husband, for the police had been back twice.

She had an unexpected, unwelcome guest one Sunday afternoon, when she was about to go for a walk. Mr. Curran answered the front door to a peremptory knock, and he showed Miss Tremblay in. He wore a scowl, as if he did not approve of the guest.

Olivia was hastily arranging the veil over her face.

"Good afternoon, Mrs. Brandon," Miss Tremblay was before her, in feathers and blood-orange satins. Olivia nodded her greeting and indicated a chair. She wondered if Miss Tremblay had seen the scars before she had draped the veil over them. *She* had no scars. Lionel had most likely never attacked her.

"I heard you had an accident. I trust you are recovered?"

Olivia readied her notepaper and pencil and scribbled the reply.

*I am well.*

"Your husband's murder was a great shock to me. I was a suspect, you know. The police seemed to think I had a hand in it. It's true I was very angry with him for marrying. He said he'd never marry. Men, how can you trust 'em? I met only one good man in my entire life—and it wasn't Lionel Brandon."

Olivia gave a polite nod. She wished that her visitor would go.

"But I must tell you why I'm here," she went on. "It's a bit delicate actually. I had a piece of jewellery—an emerald necklace—very valuable—that I had left in his home, and I cannot find it anywhere. Have you any idea of its whereabouts?"

Olivia wrote: *No, I've never seen it.*

"It was in his bedchamber, in the top drawer, in a little purple box." She eyed Olivia carefully.

*I never saw it, sorry.*

"I can't believe you haven't seen it, at least. Or maybe Annie, that servant, knows something. Where is she?"

*I don't know* she wrote. Privately she thought, *If Miss Tremblay went away for years and years, and came back expecting to find everything as she left it, she needs her head examined.* It was too much to translate into polite language and then write, so she did not.

"It must be very convenient for you not to be able to speak. I think you can speak, but pretending you're mute protects you from being investigated thoroughly in the crimes at *The Eleventh Hour*. It makes you somehow important, gives you consequence, and makes other people have consideration for you. You can speak all right. You killed Lionel. Not yourself perhaps, but you paid someone to do it. Maybe that relic who opened the door today."

Olivia's hands were still. She did not think this worthy of a reply.

"So there you are, a mute, veiled young widow. How romantic. How dignified and tragic. I will see you in prison for Lionel's murder. I shall." She rose to go. As she turned, her eye lingered on something on the mantelpiece.

Olivia followed her gaze. Miss Tremblay was looking at the snuff box.

"Do you mind if I look at that little curiosity?" she asked.

Olivia said nothing, so she picked it up and turned it over.

"Do you want this? It can't mean anything to you," she said then.

Olivia's response was to rise, take it from her and set it back in its place. Miss Tremblay tossed her head and left the room. Olivia went to the wardrobe to get her cloak for her walk.

What a horrid woman! Selfish, cruel and vindictive! What had Lionel seen in her? A reflection of himself, perhaps.

She was safe now—from him. But what of her?

Mr. Curran was waiting in the hallway as Miss Tremblay came out of Mrs. Brandon's room.

"Have you been listening at the door?" she said "It would not surprise me. That snuff box on the mantel. I should like to have it, for old times' sake. I know who left it here a long time ago, and I know you never throw anything out."

"That stays here, Miss Tremblay. Good day."

# CHAPTER SIXTY-FIVE

The nurse never arrived and Franklin, in his humble rooms, had to take on the entire care of his daughter. And what a lot of work a baby was too! Feeding, changing, bathing, laundry, and as soon as he finished, he had it all to do over again. What had happened to Mrs. Redding?

A clue emerged mid-morning. The evening before, a hackney had dropped a matronly woman off outside the house and after looking about her, she promptly changed her mind and got back in again, to return to St. Albans, she said. The onlookers had been amused because the cab driver had unloaded a great trunk and had to load it up again.

Of course. What servant who had worked in a fine house would stoop to this? A slum. Water from the pipe in the yard, no cook to send up nice meals, no shrubbery to take the baby for walks! All he had was two rooms, and one was to have been for her and the baby.

*What a fool you are, Franklin,* he said to himself, half-amused.

He could not work if he had to look after Little Livvy, as he styled her now. She was saying "BA-BA" which he interpreted as PAPA, and he was utterly proud of her. She was the best baby in the world and the brightest star in the sky! Her gowns and bonnets were getting too small for her, he'd have to buy some or get them made. He could not sew, even if he had the time!

He had to find a place where she could be minded. But who could he trust?

# CHAPTER SIXTY-SIX

Franklin, in his adventures in baby care, knew by now that every day, a child needs fresh air. When Little Livvy did not get out of the house she was listless and difficult to settle. So every clear day after breakfast, he wrapped her up warmly and set off through the streets, and she looked at everybody and everything with great interest. He stopped at a little window in Hart Street where a young lad was selling chocolate-covered nuts. Now that he was a regular customer, Charlie saved a bit of chocolate *'rocking-horse'* for the baby which he had on a teaspoon. Franklin was learning an entire new language from him too, unique to the East End of London, which he found witty and hilarious.

In the background was a veiled young woman, going about her business. What an odd sight! Veiled indoors. He supposed she was Charlie's older sister, for she had the figure of a young woman. He saw her dipping the nuts in the chocolate sauce and burned to talk to her about enrobing and such matters. He missed the factory sometimes. He missed Olivia. Where was she now? She did not know the reason he had to abandon her—to save her own nieces and nephews from hunger, and to save herself from a false accusation.

It began to rain, and he started to hurry home with the baby in his arms. As he reached the house, he saw that something was wrong. He had left the window shut and it was open now. He went inside. His rooms had been robbed, and the money he had stashed away securely under a loose floorboard was gone.

The landlord could not throw any light on it, except that a handyman he had employed some time ago, and let go because of dishonesty, had been seen in the street yesterday.

"If you can't pay your rent, you know I can't let you stay 'ere," said Mr. Jones then.

Franklin protested in the most vehement terms, but it was no use. He had to go at week's end.

"There's a place by St. Giles Church," said a neighbour to him. "It's very cheap. You can do odd jobs while a girl will tend the child for a few pennies."

On Saturday, he set off, Olivia in his arms. But he had already decided that on Monday, he would take her to the workhouse or the Foundling Hospital. He could not care for her now, and his heart was breaking.

## CHAPTER SIXTY-SEVEN

The Sisters were concerned for Olivia. They knew that the wound in her heart was infinitely worse than the wounds on her face. She could not speak. She'd written that this had happened to her before, when she was a little girl, and she thought of it as a frozen lake that her words were stuck under, and only God could get at the words.

"Olivia, perhaps you need to see the troubles others have," Sister Agatha said to her gently one day, thinking that she was brooding too much upon her troubles. "We're going down to the rookeries on Monday. Will you come with us?"

Olivia did not want to go, but she wanted to please the Sisters who had been so good to her, so she nodded.

They carried baskets for the poor, and after some time walking Olivia found herself deep in a wretched area, where the narrow alleys stank and the buildings—gin shops, pawnbrokers and hovels seemed to have trouble holding themselves up, so dilapidated were they. The people were unkempt, the children crusty-eyed and bony. Everybody was in rags. There was a listlessness about them, as if they had already passed from this life and were wraiths. She was filled with a mixture of compassion and horror. This place was worse than anywhere she had seen in Liverpool!

"There's a man with a baby in here, utterly indigent, and very ill," said Sister Sarah, descending a damp staircase to what appeared to be a little cellar deep in the ruins of a house. Sister Sarah lit a lamp to light the way.

A baby was crying. As they came into the dank cellar, with putrid material running down its walls and the overpowering smell of filth, a few shapes came into view as their eyes adjusted to the darkness. A few living creatures were crouched, without energy, around a weak fire burning in the grate.

There was a man stretched on canvas on the floor, the crying baby beside him.

"How are you today, Mr. Slater?" asked Sister Agatha.

"He's worse," said a woman from her place by the fire. He 'asn't spoke all day and the baby 'asn't been fed; there's no water."

*Mr. Slater?* Olivia thought.

"And the baby, dear little Livvy!" Sister Sarah picked up the dirty, crying infant and rocked her.

*Livvy Slater* how odd! Was it Olivia? Oliva Slater. That should have been her name if Franklin hadn't deserted her!

Sister Sarah brought the candle close to the man's face.

Olivia's heart jolted in her chest. The hair was damp on the forehead, and the face pale as death, his eyes shut and his lips cracked, but she knew him immediately.

*"Fra—!"* the sound came out, loud. Agatha looked at her curiously.

Tears streamed down her face inside her veil. She bent close to him and stroked his brow.

*Franklin, don't die! Don't!* she pleaded in silence.

She picked up a tin and looked at it closely. Powdered milk. Fresh tears fell. What terrible tragedy had befallen Franklin? Where was the child's mother?

"Do you know him, Olivia?" asked Agatha. She nodded.

She thought her heart would break with emotion as she ran up to the street to look for a man with a cart to convey Franklin out of that hell-hole. She would bring him to Hart Street.

## CHAPTER SIXTY-EIGHT

M r. Curran had a small room vacant upstairs, so Franklin was carried up there. The doctor was called, and he pronounced him dangerously ill. His fever was getting higher—if it did not break, he would die.

Olivia bathed the baby. She had helped Sally many times and was good with infants. Agatha scrubbed and sterilised the filthy bottle and made a feed. Soon the little one fell into a contented sleep in a fruit box that had been hastily covered and lined and made into a cosy little crib.

Olivia sat up with Franklin, willing him to get better, praying. She bathed his face and hands. She wore her veil in case he opened his eyes; she was sure that she was unrecognisable, but she did not want him to be startled by that leering scar on her lower cheek. How horrible it was! She debated how best to help him without letting him know who she was. She still felt a little resentment that she had been abandoned, but every time she saw the baby, she felt mollified.

No matter what he had done to her, Olivia, he didn't deserve to have come to the state that she had found him in.

His fever was getting higher, and he thrashed about restlessly, short of breath, as the night wore on. Olivia feared the worst. Then, just as a thin light came in through the curtains, he seemed to calm. His breathing became regular and he drifted into a peaceful sleep. She felt his forehead. He had cooled! He would recover!

He opened his eyes later that day and sat up. She gave him some bread and broth. She brought the baby up to see him.

She already had an idea of how to help him.

# CHAPTER SIXTY-NINE

The veiled lady in the chocolate shop was nursing him back to health. She was kind and never spoke. She was looking after Little Livvy too.

Waking from sleep once, he thought the veiled lady was the other Olivia, his lost love. But he could not see her features behind her thick netting. By Christmas, he was feeling improved, and came downstairs for a part of every day, sitting with the veiled lady and taking care of his child.

Mr. Curran was a nice old fellow. Did he know he had no money to pay him? Probably not. He worried about that. The veiled lady might expect to be remunerated in some way, but she seemed just genuinely kind. He would have to think about all this, soon, but now he was very fatigued.

One day in early January when Mr. Curran put his head around the door of his little room, Franklin asked him: "The veiled lady—may I ask her name?"

"She is Mrs. Brandon, a widow."

"I guessed that, from the black she wears. She must be in the deepest mourning to keep her face covered like that."

Mr. Curran made no reply.

"I see she makes chocolates. I used to work in a confectioners. We made many different products."

"Now tha's interesting," said Mr. Curran, coming in. "She knows something of the business, for she knew exactly what she needed when she set up 'ere. There's someone who 'elps her out, he does roasting and cracking or something, and ditching—she gets the powder and makes the chocolate syrup in the pan."

*Ollie's Chocolates*, mused Franklin. "Who's Ollie?"

"That's 'er. Olivia is 'er Christian name. You're not from this part of the country, are you, Mr. Slater?"

"I'm from Lancashire, Mr. Curran. Liverpool."

"As is Miss Coomb—I mean, Mrs. Brandon!"

*Miss Coomb!*

"She never speaks?"

"She used to. The Sisters say it was the shock of what 'appened to 'er."

"Her husband's death was sudden?"

"Sudden! I'll say it was, for 'e never saw it coming; hit from behind 'e was. *Murder.* Last March. *Beware the Ides of March.*"

"Good grief, that must have been shocking. So she stopped speaking."

"Afore that, she stopped speaking, as I understand it, she never spoke after—" here Mr. Curran stopped. "I 'ave to be getting downstairs, Mr. Slater, there's a lot of business I need to attend to. Good day."

After this conversation, Franklin was sure. But she must have forgotten him very quickly indeed, to have fallen in love and married this Mr. Brandon. The veil, the determination to hide from the world, could only mean that she was in the deepest grief— but it was also very obvious that she did not want him to recognise her. Why? His impoverished situation was awkward of course, but a little awkwardness could be got past. It was not that.

Her husband had been murdered! How horrible, what bad luck!

# CHAPTER SEVENTY

Franklin grew stronger every day and was anxious to get work. He hoped he could find work in the factory where Olivia obtained her powdered cocoa.

As for the baby, his plan had not altered from what he had decided just before he became ill. He would have to take her to the workhouse, and when he had established himself enough to employ a nurse, retrieve her. He would have to do it very soon, because he was already fit enough to work. His heart saddened at the thought of leaving her there with complete strangers. She would cry her little heart out for him. Would any of the attendants love her? It was a depressing situation.

"Mrs. Brandon," he began one day to Olivia at the breakfast table in the kitchen. The cook was out and only the two of them were there at that moment. He was eating, but because Olivia could not eat without removing her veil, she merely sat politely to keep him company.

"Mrs. Brandon, I have been trespassing upon your kindness and hospitality long enough. I have to seek work."

He received in reply a note to the effect that she had already made enquires with Mr. Wilson from whom she obtained her cocoa powder.

"How did you know I knew that kind of work?" he asked, surprised. Had Mr. Curran told her?

He saw that she was caught off guard and had no answer. Then he put his hand out towards her: "Olivia, I know it's you. Stop hiding behind that veil from me. I acted wrongly toward you, but if you only knew what I had been threatened with! Your own ruin, and the dismissal of your brother-in-law Mr. Henley—how could I have the starvation of your little nieces and nephews on my conscience? I knew you wouldn't want that."

She put her hands inside her veil, to her eyes. He continued to tell her what had happened since then. She was sobbing quietly.

"And that is my story," he finished. "But—I don't know yours, except that your husband died in tragic circumstances and that you are in deep mourning for him. I am very sorry to hear that you have suffered so."

She got up from the table and ran from the room.

Franklin got up and went in search of Mr. Curran to tell him he would be leaving very soon and that he would repay him the rent for the room as soon as he could.

He was interrupted by a series of bold, loud knocks upon the front door.

"Police! Open up!"

# CHAPTER SEVENTY-ONE

Three constables surged into Olivia's room. They began to search the cupboards, the drawers, and boxes. One constable was looking into everything—jugs, kettles, and then moved to the mantelpiece. He took up Uncle Jimmy's snuff box, opened it, and took out a piece of paper.

"Here it is, *Hart Street Pawnshop—Ticket number 48, received from Mrs. Brandon, Emerald Necklace.* Is this your ticket, Mrs. Brandon?"

She shook her head vehemently.

"Denying it, are you? The pawnbroker remembers you. A lady in a black veil, appeared to be dumb, but not deaf, understood. He gave you one hundred pounds, which you then used to hire a thug to do the job on your husband. Admit it!"

Franklin gasped and strode forward a step.

She shook her head again and shrank back, very distressed.

"You are under arrest, Madam, for the murder of your husband. Take her in."

"That's ridiculous!" exclaimed Franklin.

But he had to watch in horror as they handcuffed her.

"Olivia! You must try to speak—how can you defend yourself, if you cannot?"

She looked behind at him as they rushed her out, was there an appeal there? He could not see her eyes properly, but it must have been.

They bundled her into a police caravan.

Mr. Curran ran up to the attic. He returned staggering under the weight of dusty volumes of several thicknesses which he deposited on the hall table while he paused for breath.

"I was a legal apprentice!" he said brightly, blowing off a cobweb. "I acquired several books and kept them—just in case—and now look! I'm going to need them!"

Charlie came in a few minutes later. "Blimey O'Reilly! Oi! Aren't there any chocolates made? Where's me lady-gaffer? No pannin' done? Those twists n'twirls from Thornton's are on their way! I saw 'em up the street!"

Franklin sprang into action, put the pan on the fire and added cocoa powder and water.

"I say, 'ow do you know all that?" asked an astonished Charlie. "But where is me lady-gaffer, that is, Mrs. Brandon, gaffer being my boss, loike, today?"

"She's been arrested for her husband's murder," said Franklin rather recklessly, but he felt that Charlie would have some information and he needed information. "She didn't do it, of course; it is a big mistake."

"Of course it is, though there's them that says it was revenge, I stick up for 'er. She din't do it!"

"Revenge? For what?"

"Don't you know for what? Why she wears that veil over 'er face? Her husband knocked 'er about so bad, she 'as scars. Oh Mister, the Thorntons are 'ere." He opened the sash window, letting in a draught of cold air and the chatter of three young women.

Franklin dipped the nuts in the chocolate sauce and transferred them to the wrapping without thinking. The news had hit him like a rock dropped upon his head.

That's why she hid her face! That's why she ran from the table! And was that why she could not speak?

He had to help her, but how? Mr. Curran was in his office mumbling words like *crimen falsi* and *erratum*, clearing his throat and giving little speeches to himself or to an imaginary court. He could surely not mount a defence for Olivia. But who could?

"Oh little Miss Livvy, your Papa is an utter fool," he said, picking up the baby later and holding her up before him while she chortled. "He went to Eton with some of England's finest brains, and many of those have fathers who are quite prominent men around the Old Bailey. Shall I consult them, Miss? And will you behave for Mrs. Quinn next door for a few hours?" She loudly gurgled her approval of the scheme and dropped her rattle on his nose.

# CHAPTER SEVENTY-TWO

*Why can't I speak?* Olivia held her face in her hands.

Her veil had been taken away, and she was glad of the lonely cell. She felt very cold and desolate. She ran her hand along the ugly scars on her face. Without her veil, she felt exposed and naked. At least, nobody saw her in here.

How did the pawn ticket get into the snuff-box? It had been planted there! But who?

The people upstairs? She did not know them very well. Was it one of them?

Was it Miss Tremblay? But she would not have had an opportunity!

The front door was sometimes open during the day when tenants were coming in or out, and the children upstairs regularly left it open when they left the house—children could never remember to shut doors after them. It would be easy for someone to slip into her room while she and Charlie were having dinner or supper.

*Who?*

The day passed very drearily. She thought of Franklin and his words that very morning. He had gone away to protect her and her family! Why had he not told her before? She remembered the note she had received at Sally's home, when he had told her that he had to leave to protect her. Sally had not believed that and neither had she.

In any case, if he saw her without her veil, he would not love her anymore. She had left him in no doubt of her rejection of him, and she supposed that at this very moment, he was making plans to move from Hart Street and disappear.

It was all very hopeless. The cries and shouts and even curses of the women in the other cells was disturbing. As the day lengthened, she began to miss Franklin more and more, and Little Livvy. She thought of her now, in her long white gown and lacy bonnet, and wanted to hold her. She loved the child, had grown to love her dearly as she had cared for her. And she loved Franklin.

A bowl of broth and bread was brought to her. The warden did not take any notice at all of her scars. A prison, and a hospital, were the only establishments in London where scars were unremarkable.

# CHAPTER SEVENTY-THREE

M r. Ebenezer Bourke was astonished at his son Michael's story. Yes, he remembered young Slater—came first in the regatta three years in a row—he was now as poor as a church mouse? And he wished to befriend this Mrs. Brandon, another Liverpudlian, who had been arrested for murder? He knew the case, he had seen it in the newspapers. And she could not speak— some sort of nervous or hysterical disorder. He scribbled down everything Michael told him.

The case interested Mr. Bourke. His son assisted him in his chambers but was not yet experienced enough to take on the case, so he consented to do it. As for fees—if one could not help out a poor chap down on his luck, and that a friend, then one was hardly a Christian. A father looking after his baby daughter! It was incredible and very admirable.

"Michael," he instructed his son, "if Slater is waiting outside, tell him that he is to come and stay with us. Do not take no for an answer, we shall have a great deal to discuss. And send a note to your mother to open the Nursery!"

# CHAPTER SEVENTY-FOUR

The pawnbroker was in the witness box. He described the veiled lady who entered his shop one morning, with a small box from which she took an emerald necklace. She appeared to be mute and wrote out her name—Mrs. Brandon. He gave her the ticket and one hundred pounds.

But just before she left, she handed him a note that said:

*Do you know anybody who would commit a serious crime? Murder for instance?*

"And what was your response, Mr. Fine?"

"I told her I did not."

"Do you have the note, Mr. Fine?"

"No, she took it with her."

"Did you not feel you should alert the police?"

"I did, sir. I made a report to Constable Billings, but I was informed that since no crime had been committed, no investigation was possible."

"Prisoner to the dock!"

She was not allowed to wear her veil in court, which put her into near despair. She entered the dock with her head down, and very unhappily took questions from Queen's prosecuting counsel, a man with a biting air, and wrote down her answers to show to him.

Mr. Bourke and his son Michael were her defence, and they had somehow arranged that Franklin could sit near to them rather than to watch from the Gallery. The baby was in the care of Mrs. Bourke, a warm-hearted woman who had welcomed both into her home. Little Miss Livvy was now the darling of their household.

*Franklin can see my face*, was her thought, among others. He had tried to visit her in prison, but she had refused to see him.

She lifted her head once to survey the court, and she could see Miss Tremblay, dressed in an outfit of fiery reds and purples, her hat with feathers sky-high, bright and gaudy standing out from the others around her, mostly men and women from common walks of life, unremarkably dressed. A few journalists scribbled into notebooks. Miss Tremblay met her eye with triumph. Again, she felt ashamed of her scars.

Near Miss Tremblay sat Mr. Curran, and Olivia wondered why he had not pleaded a seat with the lawyers instead of watching in the gallery, citing his 'years of apprenticeship to the Law.' Mr. Curran gave her an encouraging wink.

"Do you deny that this is your pawn-ticket, Mrs. Brandon?" asked the prosecuting counsel.

She nodded. The grilling continued, and after it, she was weary from writing.

Mr. Bourke was up next. He had a kindly face and demeanour, but exuded knowledge and authority. She had spoken to him many times now.

"Is this your snuff-box, Mrs. Brandon?" he held up Uncle Jimmy's treasure.

She nodded, but also wrote the word *yes* for him, at his request.

"I shall describe the snuff-box for the benefit for the court," said Mr. Bourke.

"There is hardly a need for that, since she had admitted it to be hers," the Judge intervened.

"Pardon me, my Lord, but it bears a relevance to the case."

"How so?" came the snappish question from the bench. "Oh, very well."

"This is a snuff-box manufactured from African ivory and was given to a young gentleman about seventy years ago. It has a hunting scene exquisitely painted in front, and the back is inscribed with the name of the recipient, *Patrick A. Fitzgerald, 21 years 1701.* How long have you had this item, Mrs. Brandon?"

She wrote out the answer, which he read.

"Since 1856," he read.

"How did you acquire it, Mrs. Brandon?"

*It belonged to my uncle and was given to me by his next-of-kin, my mother, upon his death.* She wrote, which he read to the court.

"What was your uncle's name, Mrs. Brandon?"

Olivia bent her head to write again and handed Mr. Bourke the slip of paper.

"James O'Brien." Mr. Bourke read the name loud and clear. He repeated it—"James O'Brien."

In the Gallery, someone gave a cry, and there was a commotion. Olivia looked up. Miss Tremblay had fainted, her gloved arms hung helplessly over the balcony, her hatted head showed only its crown of feathers and bows. She was attended to and brought out.

"Was that the point of describing the snuff-box, Mr. Bourke?" asked the Judge with a little sarcasm.

"Yes, my Lord. I would like to request a recess, my Lord, for fifteen minutes."

The Judge granted his request.

# CHAPTER SEVENTY-FIVE

Miss Tremblay was sitting in a little side-room, while a matronly woman supported her head, and dabbed her face and hands with lavender water.

"Now, Lily Carter, I would enjoin upon you to tell us the truth." Mr. Curran paced the room, his thumbs in his belt.

"I didn't know she was Jimmy O'Brien's niece," sobbed Miss Tremblay. "The only good and decent man I ever met, how could I send his niece to the gallows—oh, God forgive me! That was my Jimmy's snuff box, the very one! I saw it in her room, and I asked you for it—but I thought he had just left it after him, and you, Mr. Curran, never throw anything out, *just in case*. So I thought it belonged to the room, and it never occurred to me that it belonged to her and that she was related to dear Jimmy! I'd never hurt anybody belonging to Jimmy!"

A young constable stood there, notebook and pencil in his hand, writing.

"I will put it to you, Miss Carter, that you plotted and executed this hideous crime." Mr. Curran went on. "You prevailed upon somebody to impersonate Mrs. Brandon a week before you had Mr. Brandon murdered." He wheeled around suddenly. "Have you got this, Constable?"

The constable raised a derisive eyebrow in his direction and forebore to answer, but just kept on writing.

"Yes, I did, I did! Oh, Jimmy, the only good man I ever met … I left him for a nobleman who had money—a cad—I thought he loved me, I truly did—but he cast me aside—and I was ruined! I had to earn my living in the worst possible way. After ten years, Brandon—one of my regulars—helped me to became an actress. He did not want marriage either, but he said he would never marry anybody. When I heard he married, I was furious. When I heard what he had done to his wife, I knew she would have a motive for murder. I sent my little friend Ada, in disguise, with the emerald necklace to the pawnbroker, and the note. Then I paid a boy to watch her house, and to slip in and plant the ticket where the police would find it. But he planted it in the snuff-box! And yes, I murdered Brandon—I paid someone to do it."

"Did you get all that, Constable?" asked Mr. Curran. "Did you hear Miss Carter confess to the murder of Mr. Lionel Brandon?"

"Yes, I did—I am not deaf—" said the constable testily.

"How did you know?" asked Miss Tremblay, as the handcuffs were applied to her shaking wrists.

"Mrs. Brandon showed the snuff box to me when she learned that I had known Jimmy. Your asking for it told me there was a connection between you and him. After Mrs. Brandon was arrested, I thought I would have a look through some items he did leave behind all those years ago, which I had put up in the attic, just in case. There was a likeness of Miss Carter, and she looked like you. You are Miss Carter. And some personal notes from a woman, LC."

"He should have destroyed personal notes. I fault him in that, and carelessness in leaving them behind! He did not care for me all that much, you see."

"He left in a hurry, to see to his sick and emaciated sister who had just arrived in Liverpool, the mother of Mrs. Brandon. That may excuse him perhaps."

"And you knew I would confess if I realised that his niece was for the gallows! But was there any need to do it in public?"

"It was not my decision. When I told Counsel for the Defence, they wished to do it their way. I cannot argue with men in long wigs and black cloaks."

"And if it hadn't worked?"

"She may have been convicted, perhaps."

"I saved her, then. It's the only honourable thing I have done in many years. Now I shall die. I don't care. Life is detestable in any case."

## CHAPTER SEVENTY-SIX

Olivia was relieved to breathe in the fresh air even though it was through her veil. She was free.

Franklin was by her side, and they were going to Mr. Bourke's. She would have preferred to have gone to Hart Street, but Mr. Bourke had been so kind to her, and she knew she would never be able to repay him, and now he was insisting she come to their home.

The nightmare was over! Miss Tremblay—or Miss Carter—faced the gallows for killing Mr. Brandon. According to what Mr. Curran said, she was indifferent, a mistake in her youth had led to one evil after another and she was tired of living.

She wished she could shed the name Brandon forever. Franklin was beside her; he had seen her without her veil, and he was not repulsed! He even shyly took her hand in the carriage, and she did not draw away. It was possible that they might marry after all!

The Bourke house was in a fashionable part of town, Park Lane. Mrs. Bourke made her welcome, the maid ran her a bath, and clothes were laid out for her on a soft bed.

She would have luncheon with her hosts. And for luncheon, she would have to discard the veil. She could not eat with it on. And so she presented herself downstairs as bravely as she could, her veil drawn back upon her head, and falling gently each side of her face, like a Spanish Doña, but not hiding the scars. She stole a look at Franklin before they went in. He was looking at her with such tenderness her heart filled with relief.

Everybody was happy.

If only she could speak! Why this muteness? How could Franklin marry a mute woman? What would his life be like? She was full of doubts.

They took a walk, but it was very awkward, and soon fell into silence. After she went to her chamber, she fell down by the side of her bed.

*Oh Jesus, I know you still heal today as you did when you were here on earth! Will you heal me? Will I ever speak again?*

It came to her in a rush that she had to try to forgive her husband. And Miss Tremblay. She wrestled with herself. Why should she forgive a man who had caused her face to be mutilated?

*Look at what they did to Jesus, and He forgave,* said a still, small voice.

*Oh, but He was God, it's easy for God to forgive!*

*God was also fully human. He ate, drank, wept. He was betrayed, abandoned, cursed, flogged, disfigured, and crucified ... He felt all of these as a human being does, in full ... Will you try?*

*How?*

*Keep Him close, keep your eyes fixed on Him—He will do the rest ...*

She knew that in recent times she had almost stopped praying, and when she did pray, it was only to plead for herself.

She had to begin to look outward.

The following day, Franklin said: "I have been to see Mr. Wilson. He showed me all over his factory. I like the way he runs things, but I see a great deal of room for improvement. I asked him for a position and he's going to employ me."

She was so delighted that she embraced him.

"I start next Monday. But there's another matter, Olivia. Mr. Bourke knows a doctor in Harley St. He is a specialist and has trained with a famous doctor named Broca or Brock or something in Paris, and Mr. Bourke has discussed your case with him. He's very interested in seeing you. Will you go to see him?"

She agreed, to his great relief.

The appointment was made for three days hence, and Franklin came with her.

Dr. Bellingham asked her many questions, about what she remembered from the assault that night. She wrote all the answers down.

He asked her about headaches and numbness. He was very thorough. He put a scope down her throat so far that she thought she was going to be sick. He paced the room thoughtfully and stroked his beard.

"My opinion," he said, "is that this is a different situation from what you described happened to you as a child. That was a psychological terror because your mother went away and you were lost in the woods. A very affrighted child can become *aphasic*, that is, be unable to speak for a time, long or short. It can happen in adulthood but generally it is not of long duration, or only happens in certain situations or with certain people.

"But this time, you hit your head on a hard object with great force, and you may have injured the frontal lobe—the part of your brain responsible for speech."

"The brain, Doctor? What has that to do with speech?" asked Franklin.

Dr. Bellingham pointed to a large poster with a cut-out of a brain drawn upon it. Olivia thought it looked horrible, all that grey stuff like a cauliflower!

"The brain controls every function of the body. We have only recently discovered which part is responsible for speech. Now, here is my theory, Mrs. Brandon. You injured your brain when you fell, and you were no longer able to speak anything more than rough sounds. You may have damaged that area of your brain. But it is not hopeless. Now you must apply yourself to learning to speak again, as an infant does. Until you have tried that, we shall not know whether the injury is permanent or not. You thought that this was a repeat of the aphasia you had as a child, so you did not try, or if you did, you soon gave up. Am I correct? Do not nod, or shake your head or write, try first to speak 'yes' or 'no.' He waited.

She tried, but only 'eh' came out.

"You must try to talk as much as you can. Read simple prayers and nursery rhymes aloud. At first you may suffer from fatigue. Keep trying. It's good that your headaches have abated. I will see you every week."

It was a great relief for Olivia to know that there might be a physical cause for her inability to speak. *My first words,* she promised, *will be to thank God.* Franklin held her close on the way home. He had other ideas!

He touched her forehead with his lips.

"I want you to practice two words for me," he murmured. "The words, '*I do.*' As soon as you can say those, we are getting married."

She tried to say 'yes'—a sound came out, a very little sound, like 'eek' but it was there!

# CHAPTER SEVENTY-SEVEN

"I feel like little Miss Livvy," scribbled Olivia one morning to Franklin. "Learning to talk!"

"Ah but you have the advantage! She, poor mite, only has a few words in her vocabulary—Papa, Papa and Papa." He glowed.

Olivia applied herself as the doctor ordered. It was not easy, and she was often tired. She saw the doctor every week, and he was very pleased with her progress.

She moved back to Hart Street. Charlie was very happy to see her. He had kept himself employed at odd jobs while she had been away, now he was ready to sell at the window again. Mr. Curran told her that he had almost given up on her returning, but had not let the rooms go—*just in case ...*

She wondered how she would pay the doctor. There was no obligation upon the Bourkes to pay - they had done enough *pro bono* work for her! She wished to pay rent arrears to Mr. Curran. She would have to work very hard.

But Mr. Bourke and his son were still at work on her behalf, and perhaps on their own also.

"Who represented *your* interests in the estate of your late husband, Mrs. Brandon?"

She made the word "no one" in intelligible speech.

"No-one at all? His lawyers should have. Would you like us to look into it?"

She nodded, and then remembering, said "Yes" and was happy with her own clarity. Simple words and phrases were enough for now; when she got bolder and more confident, she could add more.

The Bourkes contacted Mr. Tarrant and demanded to become acquainted with the particulars, and it ended up that there was, in fact, one thousand pounds left over when all the debts had been paid. The lawyer claimed that he had known the court case was pending, so there was no point in pursuing the interests of someone about to be hanged, and in the wake of her acquittal had been unable to contact her. True or false, nobody knew, but he handed it over now.

Olivia was overjoyed to hear this news. Now she could afford to pay them and Dr. Bellingham.

She pondered moving from Hart Street, but hesitated because she was comfortable there and business was brisk at the sash window. She also wished to keep Charlie working. He was a loyal young fellow. On the other hand, it was unfair to keep him on—he was fifteen and should learn a good trade.

*You should learn an apprenticeship*, she wrote.

"I'd like to become a baker, but I can't afford the apprenticeship money," he said.

"I—will—pay," said Olivia, smiling.

"Miss, you're speakin' again! Your voice sounds just the same as it was before! Ma will be that 'appy when she 'ears this!"

"App—rent—ish—ip?" Olivia felt excitement swell in her breast as each syllable emerged.

"Oh that too, yes, but tha' your talkin' again! Blimey O'Reilly!"

# CHAPTER SEVENTY-EIGHT

M iss Lily Carter was found guilty of murder and sentenced to hang. This made Olivia sad. She had gradually come to think of her as the woman her Uncle Jimmy had loved and had prayed for all of his life, and because she had adored her uncle, she could not bear the thought anybody he loved so devotedly should be despised by anybody who loved *him*.

Olivia wanted her to know that her uncle had always kept her in his prayers. She wrote her a letter. She did not receive a reply, but she hoped that Miss Carter went to her execution with a peaceful heart.

It did not take long for Olivia to practise the words that Franklin had especially requested, and on a fine morning in April she pronounced them perfectly in a church in Spitalfields, and the newlyweds emerged arm-in-arm to a shower of cherry blossom petals blown by a gentle breeze upon their heads.

Sally and Hughie made a special trip from Liverpool for the wedding, bringing the family with them. Olivia had prepared them all for how she would look—indeed the newspapers had carried the sensational story of the Veiled Lady Murder Trial, and even the children did not stare for longer than a moment before flinging themselves upon her with joy. Hughie was now a foreman at the warehouse and they had moved to a bigger house.

Sally was very practical. "You can wear your hair like so, curling around your face, start a new fashion! Oh am I glad you're settled and 'appy, Livvy! I din't like the sound of that Brandon. If I'd a been 'ere, I would've put a stop to it. Did I tell you that Debra has had her eighth? And she lives in a brownstone, whatever that may be, and has three servants, yes, three. Livvy, those scars are not at all as bad as you described them, and every year, they'll fade more, and din't you ever hear of pearl powder here in London? While I'm 'ere, let's you and I go shopping, and we'll find something that really covers them. Oh, I am glad to see you, Livvy! I do miss my little sister!"

Olivia felt the same. She and Sally got along famously, and Sally's humorous, though biting, take on many a London curiosity amused her.

Her brother John attended also. He had a great time in London but compared it unfavourably with Liverpool. He was a confirmed Scouser. He was doing well there, was a skilled coachmaker and was walking out with Julia Sullivan and confided to his sister that he wanted to marry her. She was a year older than him, which worried Julia, but Olivia dismissed that as a nothing, and resolved to write to her to tell her so. She was delighted at the thought of Julia becoming her sister and had no intention of allowing her to get away!

Willie was at sea at the time of the wedding. He was due into Liverpool in late May, so the Slaters went there to meet him as he only had a short shore leave. One of the days was a Sunday and they all went to church and afterwards collected around Maureen's grave and proceeded then to Uncle Jimmy's. They thought of Papa, buried far, far away. At least Debra could visit his grave. The next time they would all be together would be in Heaven. Nobody was in a hurry to get there yet. Life was good.

Two years later, Mr. Wilson retired and, having no heirs, officially adopted Franklin, who was very touched to have the chance of having a second father, and this a man who showed a great regard for him and trusted him with his affairs. Eventually he and Olivia, little Livvy and their own baby boy Thomas and their daughter Mary went to live with him in his Georgian-era house in Bedford Square. Olivia took an active part in the business, and when the shop was re-opened, she was in charge of enrobing and packing.

It took a few years, but Olivia's speech returned in full at last, and it gave Franklin the greatest pleasure to hear her read aloud to him and to his children at night. Soon, Olivia had Sally's older daughters with her to introduce them to a wider society, and they made good, happy marriages, giving Sally and Hughie some ease in their old age, though their hearts broke when their eldest son went to America at their Aunt Debra's invitation, and brought his brother out later.

Olivia's scars faded with time, and those in her heart faded also.

THANK YOU FOR CHOOSING A PUREREAD BOOK!

We hope you enjoyed the story, and as a way to thank you for choosing PureRead we'd like to send you this free book, and other fun reader rewards…

Click here for your free copy of Whitechapel Waif
**PureRead.com/victorian**

Thanks again for reading.
See you soon!

## OUR GIFT TO YOU

AS A WAY TO SAY THANK YOU WE WOULD LOVE TO SEND YOU THIS BEAUTIFUL STORY FREE OF CHARGE.

Click here for your free copy of Whitechapel Waif

### PureRead.com/victorian

At PureRead we publish books you can trust. Great tales without smut or swearing, but with all of the mystery and romance you expect from a great story.

Be the first to know when we release new books, take part in our fun competitions, and get surprise free books in your inbox by signing up to our free VIP Reader list.

As a thank you you'll receive a copy of Whitechapel Waif straight away in you inbox.

Click here for your free copy of Whitechapel Waif

**PureRead.com/victorian**